"Am I Bobby's father?"

The tears slipped down her cheeks, revealing the words her mouth couldn't form. She nodded.

Joe had suspected Bobby was his son. Kristin's affirmation only validated what he already sensed.

A part of him wanted to lash out and be angry that she'd kept their child a secret from him. But guilt came flying back in his court. After all, he'd been the one to end things that day at the ball field.

As long as he was placing blame, he'd throw some out at their fathers—hers for being so obstinate about wanting what was best for his daughter, and his for being a lowlife jerk.

But that didn't change the current fact.

Joe Davenport had a son.

Dear Reader,

Spring might be just around the corner, but it's not too late to curl up by the fire with this month's lineup of six heartwarming stories. Start off with *Three Down the Aisle*, the first book in bestselling author Sherryl Woods's new miniseries, THE ROSE COTTAGE SISTERS. When a woman returns to her childhood haven, the last thing she expects is to fall in love! And make sure to come back in April for the next book in this delightful new series.

Will a sexy single dad find *All He Ever Wanted* in a search-and-rescue worker who saves his son? Find out in Allison Leigh's latest book in our MONTANA MAVERICKS: GOLD RUSH GROOMS miniseries. The Fortunes of Texas are back, and you can read the first three stories in the brand-new miniseries THE FORTUNES OF TEXAS: REUNION, only in Silhouette Special Edition. The continuity launches with *Her Good Fortune* by Marie Ferrarella. Can a straitlaced CEO make it work with a feisty country girl who's taken the big city by storm? Next, don't miss the latest book in Susan Mallery's DESERT ROGUES ongoing miniseries, *The Sheik & the Bride Who Said No*. When two former lovers reunite, passion flares again. But can they forgive each other for past mistakes? Be sure to read the next book in Judy Duarte's miniseries, BAYSIDE BACHELORS. A fireman discovers his ex-lover's child is *Their Secret Son*, but can they be a family once again? And pick up Crystal Green's *The Millionaire's Secret Baby*. When a ranch chef lands her childhood crush—and tycoon—can she keep her identity hidden, or will he discover her secrets?

Enjoy, and be sure to come back next month for six compelling new novels, from Silhouette Special Edition.

All the best,

Gail Chasan
Senior Editor

Please address questions and book requests to:
Silhouette Reader Service
U.S.: 3010 Walden Ave., P.O. Box 1325, Buffalo, NY 14269
Canadian: P.O. Box 609, Fort Erie, Ont. L2A 5X3

Their Secret Son

JUDY DUARTE

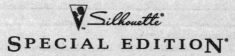

SPECIAL EDITION®

Published by Silhouette Books

America's Publisher of Contemporary Romance

To my little brother, Bobby Astleford, who over the
years has grown from a pest to a friend.

I forgive you for all those annoying things you used to do, including the times you chased me with a baseball bat. And I won't mention that night you were arrested for speeding down East Valley Parkway while
I was supposed to be watching out for you.

But setting that field on fire with a box of matches and your model car might make you famous.

I love you, Bobby.

SILHOUETTE BOOKS

ISBN 0-373-24667-6

THEIR SECRET SON

Visit Silhouette Books at www.eHarlequin.com

Printed in U.S.A.

Books by Judy Duarte

Silhouette Special Edition

Cowboy Courage #1458
Family Practice #1511
Almost Perfect #1540
Big Sky Baby #1563
The Virgin's Makeover #1593
Bluegrass Baby #1598
The Rich Man's Son #1634
Hailey's Hero #1659
Their Secret Son #1667

Silhouette Books

Double Destiny
"Second Chance"

JUDY DUARTE

An avid reader who enjoys a happy ending, Judy Duarte always wanted to write books of her own. One day, she decided to make that dream come true. Five years and six manuscripts later, she sold her first book to Silhouette Special Edition.

Her unpublished stories have won the Emily and the Orange Rose, and in 2001, she became a double Golden Heart finalist. Judy credits her success to Romance Writers of America and two wonderful critique partners, Sheri WhiteFeather and Crystal Green, both of whom write for Silhouette.

At times, when a stubborn hero and a headstrong heroine claim her undivided attention, she and her family are thankful for fast food, pizza delivery and video games. When she's not at the keyboard or in a Walter Mitty–type world, she enjoys traveling, spending romantic evenings with her personal hero and playing board games with her kids.

Judy lives in Southern California and loves to hear from her readers. You may write to her at: P.O. Box 498, San Luis Rey, CA 92068-0498. You can also visit her Web site at www.judyduarte.com.

From the *Bayside Banner:*

Wealthy property owner Thomas Reynolds made a surprise visit to juvenile court today, where he argued against the release of the fourteen-year-old who was charged with setting last week's fire that destroyed one of his warehouses on Industrial Way.

When asked by a reporter about his interest in the case, Reynolds said, "Bayside doesn't need another juvenile delinquent on the streets."

Also on hand was Detective Harry Logan, who spoke on the teenager's behalf. "He wasn't trying to be malicious," Logan argued. "His dad had been using that dilapidated building to deal drugs, and the boy was only trying to draw attention to the man's crime."

Saturday night's blaze caused Reynolds about $25,000 in damages and resulted in several fines for the condition of some of his other buildings on the street. When questioned about the faulty wiring and broken glass in the burned warehouse, as well as the other structures, Reynolds declined comment.

Chapter One

With every call to a fire, a shot of pure adrenaline coursed through Joe Davenport's blood and didn't let up until the last hot spot was out. And this one was no different.

The scent of ash filled the air as Joe walked through the charred weeds that once blanketed the vacant lot on the corner of Tidal Way and Harbor View Drive. He was searching for a point of origin and he spotted it near a melted blob of blackened red plastic.

The blaze had taken only ten minutes to contain, but the situation could have become deadly if the flames had reached the Billings place, an old clapboard house that sat next to the burned property.

Edna Billings, whose arthritis confined her to a

wheelchair, might not have escaped from the house in which she insisted upon living alone.

Dustin Campbell, a rookie fireman, strode toward Joe, his hand clamped on the shoulder of a kid who looked no more than seven years old. "We've got us a firebug, Joe. I caught him standing in the copse of trees, and he smells like smoke."

The boy wore a crisp pair of khaki slacks with dirt and grass stains on the knees. A suspicious bulge rested in the ash-smudged pocket of a freshly pressed, white button-down shirt.

"What do you have there, son?"

The towheaded boy, whose clothing suggested he'd grown up in a well-to-do home, shrugged, then reached into his pocket, withdrew a gold, monogrammed cigarette lighter and handed it over without any qualms.

Joe had no intention of scaring the kid, but a serious talk about the dangers of playing with matches or lighters, followed by an offer to make the youngster a junior fire marshal usually worked like a charm.

He'd found that instilling a bit of fear and guilt didn't hurt, either. A small flame became dangerous in the hands of a child. He assessed the boy with a narrowed eye of authority. "What's your name?"

"Bobby." The boy stood as tall as his seven-year-old stance would allow. The small, squared chin told Joe he'd have to practice his intimidation skills a bit more.

With a stubborn cowlick, a scatter of freckles across

his nose and a dirt-smudged cheek, the boy reminded Joe a lot of himself at that age.

Joe had also been a cocky, towheaded kid, prone to trouble. But he shook off the comparison. "Did you start the fire?"

"Nope." Bobby crossed his arms and shifted his weight to one side.

"But you must have seen it."

The kid nodded sagely.

Joe continued to prod for some answers and a confession. "How big was the fire when you first saw it?"

The boy used his thumb and forefinger to measure an inch. "About that big. But I didn't start it."

Joe merely nodded at the pint-size explanation that had to be a lie. "Only that big, huh? You must have been the first one on the scene."

Bobby shrugged his small shoulders in a flip defense that reminded Joe of his own run-in with the law after starting a fire in an abandoned building when he was a kid. Joe hadn't meant to do anything other than draw attention to his father's illegal activities.

His old man had been dealing crack from that warehouse for years, and Joe decided to do something about it, something that would make the firefighters and cops take notice. As a fourteen-year-old, he'd hoped the efforts of the authorities might cause a drug-addicted dad to see reason.

That day, nearly twelve years ago, had been a real turning point in Joe's life.

Once charged with arson and delinquency, Joe Davenport was now well on his way to becoming a fire chief, thanks to the guidance of Harry Logan, patron saint of bad boys.

"How do you suppose the fire started?" Joe asked Bobby.

"It was my mom's fault," the kid said in his own defense.

Now the story was getting interesting. "Are you telling me that your mom started the fire?"

"Nope. But it was her fault."

Joe remained focused and controlled, but a grin tugged at his lips. "Suppose you tell me why it was her fault."

The boy took a deep breath, then blew out a sigh, as though frustrated he had to explain something that should have been apparent. "I got a model car for my birthday, and some of the little prongs that hold the parts together broke off. I asked her if I could use her nail glue, 'cause it works good enough to stick your fingers together forever, but she wouldn't let me."

Joe raised a brow, but refrained from showing any other expression. "So she set the field on fire?"

"No. I had to figure out another way to make it stick together. Then I remembered how plastic melts, cause once I stuck a plastic fork in the fireplace and it melted into a glob that got real hard. So I took my grandpa's lighter, even though I'm not s'posed to play with it, but I was gonna be real careful." The boy's hazel eyes shimmered, and his bottom lip quivered in what looked like his first bit of remorse. "And the car caught the field on fire when it melted."

At the boy's defensive explanation, Joe considered turning his back so the kid wouldn't see him grin at a child's logic. How did parents deal with this stuff on a daily basis? This boy needed some firm, loving guidance.

Not a fist, of course, which was his own father's way of dealing with a strong-willed child. Joe wasn't an expert on child rearing, by any means, but he knew what didn't work.

"Bobby!" a woman's voice called from across the street.

So, the mother had arrived. Well, Joe had a little talk for mothers of small-fry firebugs, too. Gearing himself for a confrontation, he slowly turned around.

But nothing had prepared him for seeing Kristin Reynolds, a woman he'd dated eight years ago. She was still just as pretty as he remembered, tall and willowy, with hair the color of honey and eyes of emerald green.

The years had been good to her. *Damn good.*

She wore cream-colored slacks and a black sweater. Cashmere, most likely. And it fit nicely, showing off near perfect breasts, much fuller than he remembered.

They'd both been seventeen and balanced precariously on the cusp of adulthood when they first met.

Joe had been moonstruck that homecoming night in November. And he still found her attractive, stunning. More so, he supposed.

His heart slipped into overdrive, reminding him his blood was pumping in all the important places. There were some things time didn't change.

The pretty socialite hurried toward them, distress in her expression, an expression that looked a lot like maternal concern.

Surely, Kristin wasn't this kid's mother.

"Uh-oh," the boy muttered. He kicked the toe of his leather shoe at the dirt. "Here comes my mom."

Kristin had only recognized her son, Joe realized, because her eyes hadn't caught Joe's yet, which was just as well. He wasn't sure what to say to her anymore.

His heart thudded in his chest like a loose ball bearing, although he wasn't sure why. Anticipation at seeing her again, he supposed. And awkwardness, too. Kristin Reynolds was the first lover he'd ever had.

Joe had broken up with her after pressure from her dad, a wealthy property owner who had never forgiven the kid who set that run-down warehouse on fire and drew a ton of unflattering media attention on the condition of one of the many buildings he owned.

Thomas Reynolds had made no secret about the fact that Joe Davenport wasn't good enough for his daughter. When he went looking for Joe, demanding he stay away from Kristin, Joe hadn't backed down. Not until the red-faced man threw Kristin's happiness and her sky-is-the-limit future in his face.

At one time, Kristin had been an honor student and college-bound, but her grades had slacked and her interest in the fancy school her mother had once attended had waned.

"My daughter never lied to me before," Thomas had said, "never snuck around behind my back. And now look at her."

Joe hadn't known that Kristin had lied to her dad, nor had he known that she had to sneak out of the house in order to see him.

"Do you want to drag her down to your old man's level?" Thomas had asked.

That was the last thing Joe had wanted to do. The pompous bastard had been right, though. Kristin would be throwing her life away on a guy who would never be able to compete with her father or any of the other men in her social circle.

Joe had faked it pretty good that June day out at the ball field, when he told Kristin he didn't love her. The lie had nearly torn him in two, but her father was right. Kristin deserved so much more than what the son of a drug-dealing scumbag could offer her. And letting her go had been the right thing to do.

So why, after eight years, was he having such a heart-banging reaction to seeing her again?

Her scent, something classy and exotic—expensive, no doubt—wrapped around him like a quilt of memories on a cold and lonely night.

Joe cursed under his breath. How could she still evoke this kind of reaction in him—both emotionally and physically?

It had been eight years since he'd last held her. And it had taken ages to get over her.

"I'm okay, Mom," the boy said.

Joe looked at Bobby, and suddenly the similarities he'd seen in the kid slapped him across the face. His mind, although somewhat taken aback, did a quick calculation, starting with eight years and subtracting nine months.

The tall, honey-blond woman addressed her son. "You were supposed to be in your room, young man." When she turned her gaze to Joe, she sucked in a breath, and her lips parted in recognition.

Kristin stared at an adult version of the high school senior she'd once loved, once given her heart and virginity to. The guy who'd thrown it all back in her face and walked away.

It wasn't that she hadn't expected to see him when she returned to Bayside to spend the summer with her ailing father. She just didn't expect to see him now. Like this.

"What happened?" she asked, trying to regain her composure.

"Is this boy your son?" Joe asked.

Did he see the resemblance? Did he suspect?

How could he not? She'd been faced with the obvious every time she looked into those sweet eyes— amber-colored, like his father's.

And she'd been reminded all over again of the heartache caused by the rejection of her first and, up until recently, only lover.

It had taken years to forget Joe, but seeing him brought it all back to the forefront—the pain, the rejection, the humiliation of telling her dad she was going to have a child out of wedlock. The lie she'd told when asked who had fathered her baby.

"Yes," she said. "I'm his mother."

Joe's eyes sliced right through her usual cool and formal demeanor. And she found herself at the awkward, gangly stage again, staring in wonder at the new boy in school.

Joe had matured, filled out and grown taller. His amber eyes, more sharp and piercing than before, studied her and Bobby with a keen assessment, threatening to peel away each layer of the lie until he discovered the truth, the truth she couldn't allow to surface.

She brushed her moist palms against the hips of her slacks and prayed for a quick and easy escape. She had to get out of here, before the secret she'd kept for the past eight years muscled to the forefront.

Did Joe know?

Did he see what she saw everyday? A boy who was the spitting image of "that Davenport kid?"

Joe handed her the gold lighter she'd given her father two Christmases ago, then slid her a crooked grin. "It seems that this fire is your fault."

"Mine?" Had her voice shrieked like a fishmonger's wife? Surely not.

"That's what Bobby told us," Joe said. "He needed some glue for a model car that was broken."

"Bobby," she said, squatting to meet her son at eye level. "I can't let you play with Superglue."

"Lighters aren't a good idea, either," Joe said. "He tried to weld the plastic together."

Having a bright and inquisitive child who was prone to mischief provided her once predictable life with one adventure after another. She could only wonder what other troubles were sure to come. Her instinct told her Bobby was just an active little boy, although her fiancé suggested she'd spoiled him by being too lenient.

"Bobby, we'll talk about this at home," Kristin said. Then she looked at Joe, caught the flecks of gold in his hazel eyes, the bad-boy smile that used to make her heart go topsy-turvy.

Used to? That was an understatement.

But she couldn't allow those adolescent obsessions to interfere with her life plans. Not anymore.

For the first time in years, she'd found peace and contentment, not to mention a fiancé eager to marry her. *And not just any fiancé.*

Dylan Montgomery was a man who understood relationships, people. Children. He was a man who'd made a name for himself in the self-help market and was entering the realm of talk shows, the kind of man her father always dreamed she'd marry.

And speaking of her dad, she had his feelings to consider, as well as his health. A smoker for years, his idea of cutting back was to switch to a pipe, but his lungs were a mess and he had signs of emphysema. The overweight diabetic needed open-heart surgery, but his health complications prohibited the lifesaving procedure.

There was no way Kristin would subject him to the stress a truthful revelation would trigger at this point in his life. She might have spent the last eight years on the east coast, but that didn't mean she hadn't worried about her dad. That's why she'd come home, to be with him, to talk to his doctors. To protect him, just as he'd always protected her.

Thomas Reynolds might seem to be an overwhelming brute at times, but that was because he was a successful businessman. Rumor had it that he wasn't a man to be crossed, especially when it came to real estate sales and property development. And maybe there was some truth to that. There'd been a few lawsuits that she'd been aware of, litigations that her father had won, causing the financial ruin of at least one company. But that was business.

There was so much more to Thomas Reynolds than met the eye. He was Kristin's father—the man who adored her. The man who lugged a video cam to every school function and sat in the front row, sometimes blocking the view of others when he stood to film his daughter's attempts to perform. The man who created a goofy-looking butterfly costume for her to wear for the spring pageant, who listened over and over to her recite a poem in preparation for the elementary school speech meet.

The gentle giant who tucked her into bed each night and listened to her prayers. The brokenhearted husband who tried to compensate for his daughter's loss of her mother.

If it took the rest of Kristin's life, she wanted to make up to her father for the pain and disappointment he'd suffered because of her misplaced love and trust in Joe Davenport.

Joe touched her arm, chasing prickles of heat along her skin and jump-starting her heart. "We need to talk."

"If you're suggesting we discuss the past, there's nothing to say."

Joe looked down at her son, then back at her. "I think we have a great deal to talk about."

No way would she get into a discussion with Joe about the past, their past. Not here. Not now.

Not ever.

"I'll pay for any damages my son has caused," Kristin said. "Now, if you'll excuse me, I really need to get back home. I left the potatoes on the stove, and unless you want to be called to a kitchen fire, I'd better go check on them."

She took Bobby by the hand and started the long walk up the driveway that led to her father's estate, intent on escaping the rugged fireman's perusal and getting her son home before too many questions arose.

As she neared the house, a white three-story Victorian home built more than a hundred years ago, her lies came back to haunt her.

You're what? her father had bellowed into the phone when she called him from college to break the news.

I'm pregnant.

The day she'd intended to tell Joe that she suspected she might be carrying his child, he'd beat her to the punch by saying he didn't love her anymore. As far as she'd been concerned, there was nothing for her to do, other than leave for college a couple of months early. By Christmas break, her pregnancy had been impossible to conceal.

Who is the father? If it's that Davenport kid, I'll tear him limb from limb.

That's when her first lie went into effect, the lie she continued to perpetuate.

The baby's father is a guy I met here, Daddy. A member of the water polo team. But it was just a fling on my part. And I'm not going to marry him, no matter how hard he begs.

Her father had roared his disapproval and disappointment, but continued his financial support until she graduated with honors and took a teaching job on the east coast. Whenever her dad had suggested she come home to visit, Kristin gave him one excuse or another, prompting him to fly back east in order to see her and the grandson he'd grown to adore.

As they neared the gates that led to the house, she gave Bobby's hand a little squeeze. Not having a man around had been tough on the boy. On his mother, too. But they were doing okay. And soon Dylan would step into the paternal role. She didn't need Joe Davenport in her life.

But had he suspected the truth? She could have sworn he had. Was he still trying to sort things through? Or had he gone about his business? Put his questions aside, as she hoped he would?

Like Lot's wife, Kristin turned around, unable to hold her curiosity at bay.

Was Joe still watching?

He was.

Her feet slowed like blocks of salt, and her heartbeat reverberated in her ears. She could read the suspicion in his eyes, the questions.

Kristin's days of lying were over. But how could she tell Joe the truth without revealing the secret she'd kept from her dad for years? If her dad found out, the stress might trigger the coming heart attack that would kill him.

Maybe, she tried to convince herself, Joe would thank his lucky stars not to be strapped with child support payments and the responsibilities that came with being a parent. Maybe he'd just let his unanswered questions die a slow and easy death.

She would cling to that hope.

As Joe watched Kristin walk away, he cursed under his breath.

Was he Bobby's father?

It was definitely possible.

"That's some woman," the rookie beside him said.

Then he blew out a long, slow whistle. "She sure doesn't look like any of the mothers I ever knew."

"She's pretty, but definitely out of your league, Dustin," Joe told his younger buddy. "When a guy falls for a woman like that, the future is bound to be rocky and steep."

And there'd never been a relationship facing a more uphill battle than the youthful affair he and Kristin had innocently embarked upon.

Growing up, Joe had often been referred to as "that Davenport kid," a reference he'd tried hard to shake. Trying to live down his dad's reputation hadn't been easy. And if Harry Logan hadn't stepped into Joe's life, God only knew where he might have ended up.

The night of the fire, Harry had found Joe huddled near a Dumpster, scared out of his socks, but ready to defend his action to the death. He'd only meant to start a fire in the old warehouse, not cause a roaring blaze that would threaten other buildings on the block. But Harry had seen through the surly display of anger and zeroed in on the fear in Joe's eyes, the pain in his heart. And instead of hauling his sorry ass to juvie, as many cops would have done, Harry took Joe aside. Put him in his patrol car, but not as a suspect or criminal.

Harry had sensed that no one had ever given a damn about Joe, no one had ever listened to him. And for the next hour or so, he just sat there, nodding in understanding. Asking questions when appropriate. Listening intently, and then letting a kid who'd tried so damn hard to be tough bawl his eyes out.

And when the tears and sobs had finally stopped, Harry offered Joe something no one had ever offered him before. A sturdy shoulder to lean on. Hope for the future. A friendship with one of the greatest guys in the world. A family that included him in holiday dinners, barbecues and touch football games on the lawn. And a brotherhood of terrific guys who'd once been hell-bent misfits and now had a purpose.

Thanks to Harry, Joe had turned his life around. Still, he supposed there might be some people who couldn't forget his parentage or his shabby roots, particularly Kristin's father. But that was too bad.

Early on, Joe Davenport had made up his mind to ignore those people who couldn't quite forget who his daddy had been. And he damn sure wasn't going to spend the rest of his life proving that he was good enough for Kristin Reynolds. For one thing, her dad would never be convinced.

But things were different, now.

There was a child involved. A child Joe hadn't known about. A towheaded boy who might be his son.

If Joe was Bobby's father, he'd do right by the boy.

No matter what Kristin or her dad had to say about it.

Chapter Two

The next day, after his twenty-four-hour shift ended, Joe stood on the front stoop of the Reynolds house, preparing to knock on the carved oak door that boasted a fancy stained-glass window.

His excuse, which he hoped didn't sound lame or reveal another, more pressing reason for being here, was to talk to Bobby about fire safety and give him a junior fire marshal badge. From personal experience, Joe knew the extra effort and personal touch would help Bobby be more mindful about playing with fire.

Harry Logan and George Ellison, the fire chief who'd dealt with Joe as a kid, had used the same approach. They'd taken him to the fire station and made him feel like one of the guys. It was an experience that had turned his crappy life around and given him a purpose, not to mention a station house full of friends and, eventually, a job he loved.

Joe would have come by to talk to any other kid who'd started a fire, but the semiofficial visit wasn't his primary motive. He wanted to see Kristin again, to ask her point-blank whether he was Bobby's father.

Because if the boy *was* his son, Joe was prepared to be the kind of dad he'd always wished he had. He might not be able to make up for the lost years, but he could certainly take an active part in the future—no matter what Thomas Reynolds had to say about his involvement.

He rang the bell, then rapped on the door for good measure.

Moments later, Kristin answered, wearing a simple green dress and her hair pulled into a ponytail. She looked young, much like the teenage girl she'd once been. The girl he'd once loved.

When she saw him, her emerald eyes widened and her mouth dropped. Obviously, she hadn't expected him to follow her home.

He never had before.

Mostly because she hadn't wanted him to.

But things had changed, now that they'd grown up and gone their separate ways.

"Joe," was all she said, her voice soft, wispy. She blanched for a moment, then seemed to recover.

"I came to talk to Bobby." *And you.*

"Bobby went on a picnic to Oceana Park with the family who lives next door. They won't be home until later this afternoon."

"I'm sorry I missed him." Joe's words weren't entirely true. What he and Kristin had to talk about was best done in private, out of Bobby's hearing range.

"Thank you for stopping by," she said, as though wanting to send him on his way.

But Joe wasn't about to be put off. "Like I said before, Kristin, you and I have some things to discuss. And I thought now might be a good time."

She glanced over her shoulder and, before Joe could broach his main question, she took his arm and led him across the manicured lawn to the silver Chevy Tahoe he'd parked in the drive. "Now's not the right time."

Because her father was home, no doubt.

Would Thomas Reynolds always stand between them like an armed sentry? Or a rottweiler with eyes glazed and teeth bared?

Joe crossed his arms over his chest, his gaze snagging hers and demanding the truth—the real reason why *now* wasn't a good time to talk. "What's the matter, Kristin? Afraid your father will see me on his property and come running with his shotgun?"

"No, of course not."

Joe didn't believe her. The lie she'd uttered had brought a blush to her cheeks and a splotch to her throat and neck. She was afraid her dad would raise hell.

Well, he would just cut to the chase. "All right, Kristin. I'll go. For now. But answer one question. Am I Bobby's father?"

Her lips pursed, and she crossed her arms in a defensive stance. "Bobby isn't your concern."

"If he's my son, he is."

She stood there, silent and cool as a Grecian statue, yet Joe had the feeling an unexpected gust of wind would blow her over and smash her to smithereens.

For some insane reason, he felt an urge to comfort her, to wrap her in his arms and pull her close. Tell her she could depend on him for support.

But Kristin Reynolds, soft and gentle as she was on the outside, had an inner strength Joe had always admired. So instead of giving in and offering the protective gesture, he held firm. "I want some answers. And I'm not going away until I get them."

She turned her back, as if to stomp off, but her feet remained rooted to the driveway. Was she crying? Considering a response? Trying to decide on how to tell him the truth?

Or was she merely going to recite the trespassing laws? Remind him that he'd never been welcome on Reynolds property?

Trying to gain control of her emotions, Kristin brushed a tear from her eye and stared at the front porch of the house in which she'd grown up, the home that had offered her refuge, comfort and safety over the years.

As much as she'd hoped Joe wouldn't show any interest in her son, she knew the cocky, take-charge fire-fighter wouldn't be put off.

What a sticky wicket she'd found herself in now.

She'd told Joe that she wasn't afraid her father would come chasing after him with a shotgun. And she wasn't. Her father wasn't a violent man, although he'd been known to raise his voice loud enough to cause people to tremble when he'd been crossed.

But Joe's presence and the subject he wanted to discuss would cause Thomas Reynolds to rant and rave, which, God forbid, could trigger the heart attack that might kill him.

Joe took her by the hand, turned her to face him. "I want a blood test to establish paternity."

Kristin blew out a weary sigh. The stubborn fireman was taking this too far. She had to tell him something. The truth, she supposed. But not until she could get his promise. His promise to keep her secret until it was safe to reveal.

She swiped at a loose strand of hair that had slipped free of her ponytail and tickled her cheek, then gazed at the angular face of the man who had such power over her—power to turn her knees to jelly, her heart to mush. Power to turn her life upside down and blow her relationship with her father to hell.

"Slow down, Joe. There's a lot you don't know, a lot you don't understand. I'll discuss it with you—in private—if I can get your word about something."

"What's that?"

"You'll have to promise to keep our discussion a se-cret until I say it's okay."

Joe had a stubborn pride and a sense of honor. If he gave her his word, he'd keep it. She doubted the years had changed that about him.

She watched him contemplate what she'd said, the stipulations she'd lined out. And she wondered what would unfold if he accepted her terms.

After what seemed like ages, but was probably only a minute or so, he dragged a hand through his wheat-colored hair. "All right. I'll play it your way."

Relieved, Kristin slowly let out the breath she'd been holding. "Okay. But I don't want to discuss this sub-ject here."

"How about we talk about it over dinner tonight?"

Dinner? That wasn't what she had in mind. It seemed too much like a date. Just the idea of being alone with Joe Davenport again brought forth a rush of heated memories. Shared chocolate shakes at Dottie's Diner, hands entwined under the table. Slow dancing under the strobe lights at the Spring Fling. Stolen kisses behind the dugout at the baseball field.

She tried to focus on the day he'd broken her heart, the day he stopped loving her. All the nights she'd cried herself to sleep. Anything but the attraction she still felt for a guy who'd thrown her heart back in her lap.

Joe slid her a grin. "I know a quiet little out-of-the-way place where even James Bond would feel comfort-able spilling his secrets."

Secrets. She'd kept hers so close to the vest that she wasn't sure she could share them with anyone.

What did Joe expect from her, after all these years?

The truth, she supposed. Lord knew she was tired of the lies, the deceit. But not tired enough to risk her dad's health.

"Give me the directions," Kristin said, "and I'll meet you there."

"You don't want me to pick you up?" Joe's jaw tightened, and his eyes narrowed. "Your dad always stands between us, doesn't he?"

Yes, he probably always would, but there was no need to get into that discussion now. "You never did like to play by anyone else's rules."

"I still don't." He withdrew a notepad from the dash of his Tahoe, then scratched out an address. "I'll meet you at four-thirty. Before the dinner crowd shows up."

She nodded, then stood in silence as he climbed into his SUV and drove away.

At four-fifteen that afternoon, Kristin borrowed her father's Lincoln Town Car and drove to Harbor Haven, a small seaside enclave twenty miles north of town.

As a teenager, she'd had to sneak out many times to see Joe Davenport. And it seemed as though history were repeating itself. She'd told her dad that she wanted to meet an old friend, which was true. Thank goodness he hadn't asked for a name.

Other than the secret she'd kept for years, Kristin hadn't lied to her dad since she and Joe had broken up. She'd always valued honesty. And the deceit clawed at her heart and conscience. But she didn't know how to backpedal now; the lie seemed to hold her firmly in place.

She looked in the rearview mirror, checking her appearance in spite of her resolve not to do so. An hour earlier, she'd actually found herself primping before the bathroom mirror, trying to look her best.

A glance at the bed, where several different dresses and outfits lay, had made her realize the foolishness of her girlish behavior.

She and Joe were merely old friends. Nothing more, nothing less. And she certainly didn't want him to think she still had the hots for him.

The memory of their breakup was still etched deeply in her mind. It still haunted her dreams. Still brought a familiar ache to her heart, a watery blink to her eyes, if she'd let it. For the most part, the past was over and done. She had a rosy future in front of her, and risking another broken heart wasn't in her game plan.

After putting aside any romantic misconceptions, she'd finally chosen a pair of black jeans and a yellow sweatshirt. This was a casual meeting by the beach, not a date. And she wasn't about to give her old lover the impression that she thought it was anything else.

She gazed out the windshield, following Joe's directions until she found The Gull's Nest, a quaint eatery that offered outdoor dining. Joe had been right about the place. It was out of the way and quiet.

Before parking the car, she spotted him sitting at a table outside, wearing faded jeans and a black T-shirt. He'd dressed casually, too. Thank goodness.

Yet he was still too darn attractive for his own good.

Those amber-colored eyes watched every step she made, until she reached the table where he waited, feet stretched out before him in that sexy stance he'd probably never shake.

He stood, while she took a seat.

"Thanks for coming out here to meet me," he said.

She merely nodded.

A matronly waitress handed them menus, then asked if she could get them a drink.

Kristin thought an iced tea or soda might be best, but chose white wine for its calming effect. Joe ordered a beer.

"It's pretty here," she said, trying to avoid the topic they'd both come to discuss.

"I thought you'd like it."

Rather than look at the sandy-haired man who studied her intently, she glanced at the setting sun, which had painted a colorful sunset. The kind made for artists. And lovers.

A summer breeze stirred the salty ocean air, and seagulls cried and frolicked on the shore. An aura of romance settled upon the table, as did a gentle yet heavy silence.

Kristin had expected Joe to throw his question out, like a fisherman casting his nets upon the sea. But he kept both his question and his thoughts to himself. For that, she was glad.

It wasn't until after the waitress delivered their drinks that Joe finally spoke, finally began to lay his thoughts on the line. "I realize a lot has happened in the past eight years."

More than he'd previously suspected, that was for sure, but she let him speak. Let him sort through his thoughts and open his case.

"I don't have any right to demand anything from you," he said, "but if Bobby is my son, I deserve to know."

He was right, but before she could gather her courage, try to explain, the waitress returned to take their order.

They both asked for the fish tacos, which were the house specialty. Kristin hoped the chatty waitress would remain, pull up a seat and join them. Anything to prolong the moment of truth.

When the woman took their orders back to the kitchen, Joe continued. "You left town right after our breakup. You weren't scheduled to go until August."

That was true. But how could Kristin have stayed in town, heartbroken and pregnant with Joe's baby? She'd had to leave before the secret was out. She'd loved Joe with all of her heart and soul. Breaking up with him had nearly torn her apart, and she wasn't about to let her dad know she was hurting, that she'd been jilted. God only knew how he would have reacted.

She'd told Joe her father wasn't a violent man, and he wasn't. His battles were usually fought at a conference table or, when necessary, in court.

But back then, if faced with a pregnant teenage daughter, he might have stormed after Joe, pressed charges of some kind. Made Joe's life miserable. So, in a way, leaving had been a means of protecting both of the men she loved.

"My mother's sister lives back east," Kristin said. "So when Aunt Mary invited me to spend some time with her before I started school, I jumped at the chance. Getting out of town seemed like a good idea. Believe it or not, I cared about you. And when you told me you didn't love me, I was crushed."

Again, Kristin relished being able to speak the truth. She hadn't told anyone about Joe, about their relationship, about her heartbreak. And for once, it felt therapeutic to let the words out. Liberating.

"Did you leave town pregnant? With my baby?" His eyes drilled into her, his words hammered on her heart.

"I've never discussed Bobby's father with anyone," Kristin said, "and I won't do so now, unless I can get you to promise me something."

"It's a simple question, Kristin. Just give me a yes or a no."

Answering *no* would be so simple. So easy. But she wasn't about to lie about Bobby any more than she had to. But neither was she willing to jeopardize her father's health.

"Things aren't simple, Joe. I've kept secrets from my dad, secrets that will anger him when he finds out. And I'm not ready to confess yet." She took a sip of wine, enjoyed the cool taste as it slid down her throat. Then she studied the fireman across from her, the man who'd once turned her inside out and promised to do so again, if she let him get too close.

Thank goodness she knew better than to allow that to happen. She needed a man who could commit for the long haul.

"They say confession is good for the soul," Joe said.

She nodded. "I'm sure you're right. But my dad has serious health problems. He needs bypass surgery, but other complications—his weight, sugar diabetes, the early stages of emphysema—have the doctors debating whether he can handle the surgery. I want to keep his life stress-free until the cardiologist and other specialists can determine a treatment."

Joe's jaw tensed, and she feared he was digging in his heels for a battle of attrition. Was he unwilling to understand, to care about her dilemma, her personal stake in all of this?

"I'm not into secrets," he said.

She knew that. That's why she'd never told Joe about having to sneak out to meet him. "I'll tell my dad the truth, but I don't want him finding out until I think his health can handle it."

"So what are you asking me? Not to tell your father?"

"I'm asking that you honor my secret and my privacy.

If I share that information with you, I want you to promise not to tell anyone until I say it's okay."

Before Joe could speak, the waitress brought their food. The silence was almost overpowering, as Kristin awaited Joe's decision.

She studied her plate and poked at her food. But it wasn't just nervousness and a guilty conscience that made her stomach all atwitter. It was the sandy-haired man across the table, the man she'd never been able to shake from her blood. Or her heart.

Time heals, the old adage said. But did it? Why did her old lover continue to stir up feelings and desires she'd buried years ago?

A wave of guilt splashed over her, as she thought about Dylan, her fiancé. He was a good man. Solid. Dependable. Willing to make a commitment. Yet, if truth be told, he didn't stir the same fire that Joe did.

But there was more to life than hot sex. And quite frankly, a warm, dependable soul who would stick by a woman through good times and bad would prove to be invaluable in the years to come.

"Okay, Kristin. I promise to keep your secret." His gaze cornered her, demanded to hear the words. "Am I Bobby's father?"

The tears slipped down her cheeks, revealing the words her mouth couldn't seem to form. She nodded her yes.

Joe had suspected Bobby was his son. Kristin's affirmation only validated what he already sensed. He could tell by looking, by some kind of built-in parental instinct, maybe.

A part of him wanted to lash out and be angry that she'd kept their child a secret from him. But guilt came flying back in his court. After all, he'd been the one to end things that day at the ball field. And he'd made it clear he didn't want to see her again. He couldn't blame her for staying away.

And as long as he was placing blame, he'd throw some out at their fathers—hers for being so obstinate about wanting what was best for his daughter and his for being a low-life jerk.

But that didn't change the current fact.

Joe Davenport had a son. A boy who was a lot like him.

And for some reason that didn't make any sense whatsoever, it pleased him to know he and Kristin had made a baby.

He'd loved her so much back then. Of course, that was before he knew how much her father hated him, how star-crossed their relationship had been. Still, their short time together had been good—almost magical— while it lasted.

And they'd made a baby.

"Think it happened out at the lake, that afternoon?" he asked. "Or at the cabin in Julian?"

"Huh?"

His question seemed to take Kristin aback, as though she'd forgotten about the day she'd first given herself to him.

"We only made love a couple of times," he continued. "And I guess it really doesn't matter when Bobby
was conceived."

"It was at the cabin," she said, her voice soft and gentle. "I'm not sure how I know, but—"

"You're probably right." Joe had that same feeling.
The day had been special. Perfect. And if God chose to
bless the world with a new baby, that would have been
the time.

A sappy grin rose to the surface, and he couldn't
stop the excitement that bubbled inside. He wanted to
be the kind of father he'd missed having. A father like
Harry Logan, who always had time to listen, time to advise. Time to throw back his head and laugh, to enjoy
an afternoon with his family, even if that family included a bunch of onetime bad boys like Joe.

Yep, Joe wanted to be that kind of dad to Bobby. He
wanted to have backyard barbecues and toss footballs
around on the grass. He wanted to take his boy fishing.
And teach him how to ride a bike, if Bobby didn't know
how already. They'd play catch. And—

Kristin kept brushing the tears from her eyes.

Sheesh. Was she unhappy about telling him? Or sorry
she'd kept the secret? Joe wasn't sure what broke the
floodgates, but he felt responsible. He reached across
the table and took her hand. "I'm happy about this."

She looked up at him, surprise splashed across her
face. "You are?"

"Yeah." He shot her a smile that he hoped would

help ease her mind, in one way or another. "I like the idea of having a kid."

"But you understand, we have to take this slow. Right?"

"Yes," Joe told her, "but I want you to understand something, too."

"What's that?"

"I might have agreed to hold off announcing my fatherhood, but that doesn't mean I don't expect to be involved in my son's life."

She nodded. "I understand."

"Starting immediately."

"What do you mean?" She pulled her hand back, and her eyes widened. "You promised not to say anything."

"I won't. I'll keep the secret. But I didn't say anything about staying away. I'll start off by being his friend, you know, a fireman who took an interest in a fatherless boy."

She seemed to relax, to accept his compromise. "I suppose that will work."

"Some guys might not like a surprise like this, Kristin. But I'm not just any guy. I want to take an active part in Bobby's life. And I plan to be the best dad in the whole world."

She fingered the stem of her wineglass, then looked at him. Lord, she had the prettiest green eyes he'd ever seen. He'd missed gazing at her.

"But this is a secret for now," she said.

"For now." Joe shot her a smile. "But we're going to tell Bobby. Soon."

"When the time is right," Kristin insisted. "You promised to let me decide when that would be."

He had, although he was having cold feet about the promise. Still, he owed her something. He'd gotten her pregnant, then told her he didn't love her anymore, left her to fend for herself and the baby.

Yep. He owed her something. And he'd given his word to keep quiet until she said the time was right.

But as far as he was concerned, that day couldn't come too soon.

Thomas Reynolds might not think Joe was good enough for his daughter. And maybe he was right. But Bobby was a Davenport.

Once upon a time, Joe might have backed down when it came to a relationship with Kristin. But this was different. He wouldn't bow out of his son's life. Not now. Not ever.

Kristin and her father had better brace themselves, because Joe Davenport was going to be a father to his son.

And he would fight whoever got in the way.

Chapter Three

Kristin knew Joe meant to be a part of Bobby's life, but she hadn't expected him to show up at the front door on his next off-duty day, wearing a white T-shirt, a pair of faded jeans and a smile that battered the wall she'd built around her heart.

"I came to see Bobby," he said.

She fought the urge to look over her shoulder, to see who had seen him at the door. But she didn't dare peek; she didn't really need to. Her father's room was on the backside of the house, and he was busy on the Internet this morning, dabbling with his online stock purchases.

Besides, as a fireman, Joe's interest in Bobby seemed reasonable. Her father couldn't find any fault in that.

"I'd like to take Bobby to the station and introduce him to some of the guys. You know, let him see the equipment. Get a private tour."

When he flashed her another crooked smile, she couldn't help but relax. Somewhat.

For some crazy reason, she wished she'd known he was coming so that she could've run a comb through her hair, put on some lipstick.

But Joe had come to see Bobby, not her. And she had no business primping for her old lover. Not when she'd already been burned by him and his change of heart. And not when she had a commitment to someone else.

Kristin called her son, and moments later Bobby came bounding downstairs.

"Uh-oh." The little boy slowed his steps when he laid eyes on the off-duty fireman on the stoop. "I haven't been playing with the lighter anymore."

"That's good," Joe said. "I came by to talk to you about fire safety and doing me and the guys down at the station a favor."

"You want me to do a favor for you?" Bobby's eyes grew wide. "Sure. What is it?"

"We'd like you to represent the fire department while you're at school. You know, by telling the kids about the dangers of playing with matches and lighters. After all, you've seen what happens when a fire gets out of hand."

Bobby broke into a full-on grin. "Cool."

"Of course, I'd make you a Junior Fire Marshal," Joe

said, "so the kids know you've been trained and certi-
fied by the department."

"That's way cool." Bobby made his way to the front
door and gazed at the man he didn't realize was his
daddy with such admiration, such awe, such respect,
that Kristin had to swallow a lump in her throat and
blink back tears.

Joe shot a glance at her. "If it's all right with your mom,
I'd like to take you down to the station this morning."

A part of her wanted to hold Bobby tight, to keep him
away from his father. To keep the future from unfolding
without her. But she couldn't say no.

The idea of those two peas in a pod taking off without her didn't sit well, though. She'd love to witness
their first father-son experience and longed to see them
together, to watch their reactions. But she'd better con-
jure an excuse other than the truth.

"I've never had an official tour of a fire station," she
said, trying to make her interest sound as though it had
nothing to do with father and son. "Can I go along, too?"

Joe studied her for a moment, his thoughts impossible
to read. Then he shrugged and slid her a half smile. "Sure."

Had her request surprised him? Bothered him? She
wasn't sure, but something told her he was merely being
polite for her son's sake.

For *their* son's sake.

Her secret had become his secret, and she hoped he
would honor it until she deemed the time was right to
reveal it.

"If you'll excuse me," she said. "I'll get my purse."

Moments later, they all climbed into his Tahoe and started down the road. Bobby sat in the middle of the spacious backseat, as eager and excited as Kristin had ever seen him.

How strange, she thought. To be riding down the street in Joe's SUV. Like a family on the way to the amusement park. Or to the movie theater, the mall or the beach.

It seemed so right yet, at the same time, surreal.

Kristin found it difficult not to glance across the seat at the tall, rugged man behind the wheel. Impossible to ignore his square chin, the quirk of his smile, the glimmer in his gold-flecked eyes.

Even when she looked straight ahead, she couldn't help but relish the smell within the cab of his vehicle, a combination of new car and Joe's light, musky aftershave.

But Kristin wasn't the only one having trouble keeping her eyes to herself. Joe kept glancing at Bobby, at his hair, his face. The little hands that rested upon small knees.

Was he taking inventory? Checking the Davenport contribution to the boy?

Kristin found Joe's interest heartwarming, but at the same time scary. She'd never had to share Bobby before and she refused to consider the thought of cross-country visitation. It was more than a mom could handle at this point.

When they reached the station, Joe parked in back, next to a white Jeep Wrangler and a blue Ford Explorer. "We're here."

"All *right!*" Bobby's enthusiasm was hard to ignore.

And so was her own nervous excitement. She hadn't been to visit Joe's home away from home in years.

Joe watched Kristin and Bobby climb from the Tahoe. He'd intended to spend time with his son alone, and Kristin's request to join them had taken him by surprise. Didn't she trust him to be alone with Bobby? They'd made a deal, and she ought to know he'd abide by it. For the time being, anyway.

Of course, having her come along wasn't so bad. In fact, it was kind of nice. Made him almost feel like part of a family.

But if he knew what was good for him, he'd stop thinking about stuff like that.

Things between him and Kristin had ended a long time ago, and he had no intention of resurrecting something destined to crash and burn. Especially with a woman who would choose her father over him every time.

And Thomas Reynolds wasn't just any man, any father. The hard-ass real estate tycoon had pulled a few political and financial favors and fought to thwart Harry's efforts to gain leniency in Joe's case. He'd argued that Bayside didn't need another known juvenile delinquent back on city streets. Joe wasn't so sure that Reynolds wasn't just trying to get back at him personally, because the wealthy businessman hadn't spoken in juvenile court since.

Fortunately, the judge had seen the results of Harry's

involvement with other troubled young boys and ruled in Joe's favor. But Joe had a feeling Reynolds had never gotten over the court's decision.

And Joe doubted he ever would.

There wasn't much the wealthy landowner did that Joe didn't pay close attention to. And more than one Bayside citizen had crossed Thomas Reynolds, only to meet with financial ruin somewhere down the line. A coincidence? Joe didn't think so.

Shoving aside his resentment of Kristin's father, he placed a hand on Bobby's shoulder. "Come on, I'll introduce you to my family."

The first fireman they met was Sam Henley, a five-year veteran on the squad. "Hey, Davenport. What's up?"

Joe gently squeezed his son's small shoulder and addressed his friend and fellow firefighter. "I brought along a candidate for that Junior Fire Marshal position. His name is Bobby."

"It's nice to meet you, son." Sam extended a hand in an adult greeting that caused the boy to beam with pride. Then he cast an appreciative eye on the attractive woman at Joe's side.

"This is Kristin Reynolds," Joe explained, "Bobby's mother."

After pleasantries were made, Sam gave Bobby and his entourage a full tour of the station, the trucks and equipment.

The guys Joe thought of as brothers kept glancing at him and Kristin with knowing looks. Joe could tell by the way they grinned at him—and winked when Kristin wasn't looking—that they assumed his interest in the boy had more to do with the pretty mother.

Maybe, to an extent, they *had* sensed something. Being this close to Kristin again was having an effect on him. And try as he might, he couldn't seem to keep from gazing at her, appreciating the attractive woman at his side.

She wore a turquoise silk blouse that set off the color of her eyes, made them glimmer and sparkle. The slinky material dressed up a simple pair of black jeans that hugged her hips. Kristin had always been attractive, but the years—or maybe motherhood—had done something to her. Made her blossom.

As her shoulder brushed against him, he fought a natural urge to take her hand or to slip an arm around her and pull her close. To go back in time and take up where they left off.

It was a stupid thought. What they had before had been special—but the situation had been hopeless. And now, eight years later, they'd both grown up. Changed more than either of them could probably guess. And if that weren't reason enough to ditch the sappy urges, there were too many secrets between them. Too much pain. Too much reality.

Kristin was destined for bigger things than a small-town life with an average Joe.

No. His interest was in his son. And Joe looked forward to the day he could announce that relationship to the world.

* * *

After the tour of the fire station, Joe took Kristin and Bobby to lunch at Burger Bob's, a nearby hamburger joint with an indoor playground to attract kids and families.

Bobby zipped off to play until their order was ready, while Kristin waited with Joe at a corner booth.

It felt funny sitting across from her old teenage lover, waiting for a meal of cheeseburgers, fries and chocolate shakes—fare that had once been their favorite.

And it felt even stranger to go out to eat with their son, something other families did on a routine basis.

"Thanks for letting me take Bobby to the station," Joe said.

She smiled, remembering how much time Joe had spent with the fire department when he was a teen, how the firefighters became the family he didn't have. She supposed it was a way for Joe to introduce his son to his world. And she was glad she was able to share the day. "Thanks for letting me tag along."

"You're welcome." He shrugged. "It was no big deal. Just a visit to the fire station. Kids like that sort of thing."

She suspected it was much more than that. Unless things had changed, the department was Joe's life, his family, his home. And taking Bobby to meet his buddies and see the station was an attempt to share himself with his son. But Kristin didn't comment.

Nor did she mention the fact that he'd once shared his life at the station with her. And that she'd been honored when he had.

She remembered how his eyes had lit up when he told her about the camaraderie he found with the firemen. In fact, his anecdotes had made the guys down at the station seem so real, so extra-special, that she'd really wanted to meet them herself.

He'd taken her to the fire department once to introduce her to his friends. Most of the guys had been out on a call, but the ones she'd met had made her feel welcome. And special.

The aroma of burgers and fries filled the air, as they sat at the white Formica table, the past hovering too close, the future just out of reach.

When one of Burger Bob's employees brought a tray of food and set it down, Kristin called Bobby to eat.

"Aw, do I have to?" the boy asked.

Kristin was ready to begin the usual argument, whenever her son wanted to continue playing instead of going to bed, brushing his teeth or eating dinner, but Joe stepped in.

"Bobby, a fireman has to eat when the chow is in front of him, since he never knows when he'll be called out on an emergency that could keep him away from the station for hours."

The boy nodded, then joined them at the table, taking a seat next to Joe. More than once, his eyes flitted back and forth between his messy, ketchup-laden burger and the man he'd obviously come to admire.

"Do you have a family?" Bobby asked Joe. "You know, kids and stuff?"

Both adults paused, hands half-raised or half-low-ered, jaws frozen.

"The guys down at the fire station are my brothers," Joe said. "And I've got a friend named Harry, who has included me in his family."

Joe shot a glance at Kristin, and she bit her bottom lip.

She could read the pain in his eyes, the accusation. The disappointment. He wanted her to tell Bobby now, to use this as an opening to explain. But she couldn't allow it. Her son might tell her father.

No more lies, she'd promised herself. But she couldn't help this lie of omission.

What a web she'd woven.

As Joe munched on a double bacon cheeseburger, Bobby studied him while sucking chocolate shake through a straw. "For an adult, you're pretty cool."

"Oh, yeah?" Joe answered, a grin tugging at his lips. "Thanks."

"You're even more cool than Dr. Dylan."

"Dr. Dylan?" Joe asked. His eyes traveled to Kristin, and she felt her cheeks warm.

Her fiancé, Dylan Montgomery, was better known as Dr. Dylan. And it was no surprise to her that Bobby would like Joe better. Dylan hadn't taken Bobby on any outings—yet, although she was sure he would one of these days. Dylan's book tours and speaking engage-ments took up a lot of his time.

"He's not a shot-and-medicine kind of doctor," Bobby said. "He's on TV."

"A movie star?" Joe asked.

"No," Bobby interjected before Kristin could explain. "Not like that. Dr. Dylan just tells other people what they're doing wrong."

Joe looked at Kristin, then questioned the boy. "Does your mom take you to see Dr. Dylan?"

"Nope. He comes to our house, sometimes. He's my mom's boyfriend."

"I see," Joe said.

So, pretty Kristin hadn't been a hermit. Or celibate. But then, neither had Joe. But for some reason, it prickled him to know she had a boyfriend.

Because of his son, he told himself. That's the only reason.

But maybe he was just plain envious of the guy who'd captured Kristin's heart. Envious because Dr. Dylan represented the kind of man Thomas Reynolds approved of as a son-in-law.

Bobby popped a French fry into his mouth. Between chews, he said, "Dr. Dylan is stuffy."

"Stuffy?" Joe asked.

"That's what Megan, my sitter, says. I'm not sure what it means, but I think it's because he reminds her of my stuffed walrus."

Kristin choked on a fry—uncomfortable with the table topic?—then cleared her throat. "Looks like I'm going to have to talk to Megan. I don't think Dr. Dylan looks like Wally the Walrus."

"He has that funny mustache," Bobby reminded

her. "And his chest and neck get all poochy when he talks."

"You've always liked Dr. Dylan," Kristin said. A blush on her cheeks suggested the conversation had taken an uncomfortable turn.

"I do." Bobby looked at Joe and laughed. "I like Wally the Walrus, too."

Joe couldn't help but chuckle. He wondered whether he should correct the kid, but for what? Being honest? Having an opinion? Heck, he didn't need to lay eyes on the guy to share the stuffed-walrus opinion.

Bobby pushed the remnants of his burger aside. "Can I go play now?"

"One more bite," Kristin responded.

The boy complied, then dashed toward the multicolored climbing structure, leaving Joe and Kristin alone. Joe took the opportunity to learn more about Dr. Dylan, to find out how Kristin felt about the man. How deep their relationship went.

But only because the man might become his son's stepfather, Joe told himself. That was the only reason. Yet he couldn't ignore a tinge of envy.

"So, tell me about Dr. Wally."

Kristin clicked her tongue. "Stop that. His name is Dylan. And he doesn't look like a stuffed walrus."

"Okay. Tell me about Dr. Dylan."

She arched a brow. "Why do you want to know about him?"

"Just curious."

She scrunched her nose, and Joe assumed she felt awkward discussing her new lover with her old one.

He supposed it felt kind of weird to him, too, but like a puppy with a brand-new slipper in his mouth, he couldn't seem to leave it alone. "Is he good to you?"

She nodded. "And he's good to Bobby, too. Although he says I'm too easy on him."

"Are you?"

"Bobby seems to get into a lot of trouble, but sometimes I find it kind of funny. Or clever. The other day, he took the closet doors off the runner, leaned them against the shelf and made a slide in the bedroom." She fiddled with the straw in her drink. "I scolded him, of course, but didn't give him time-out."

Joe's old man would have found that reason to bounce Joe across the room. Kristin's method of discipline seemed in line with his own.

"Dylan thought Bobby was being destructive. But the doors had already been broken, and I was waiting for the handyman to fix them. I thought Bobby was just bored. And a little creative."

"I agree." Joe reached across the table, took her hand in spite of his resolve not to get too touchy-feely. "Bobby's a great kid, Kristin. You've done a good job raising him by yourself."

He didn't mention being sorry that he couldn't have been there for her. Or that he placed a lot of the blame on her dad.

It was all water under the bridge now, he supposed, but the fact was, Joe didn't like Thomas Reynolds any more than Thomas liked him. And Kristin would have eventually resented Joe for coming between her and her father.

As they nursed their chocolate milkshakes, drinks they'd shared in the past, Joe couldn't help wondering how their lives would have turned out had he not buckled to her father's demands and let Kristin go.

Would she have told him about the baby? Would they have run away and gotten married? Lived in a crummy apartment, the only place he would have been able to afford?

He shook off the curiosity. Kristin, who'd only known wealth and privilege, wouldn't have been happy with the simple life Joe could provide. And even though his paycheck was now considerably larger than what it would have been eight years ago, what they once had was over and done.

His only concern was Bobby. For the boy's future. And making sure he got to spend as much time as possible with his son.

"How long will you be in town?" Joe asked her.

"For the summer, I think. Assuming my dad's health improves, I'll return to the east coast when the new school year starts."

That gave Joe some time to bond with his son, time to get to know him. Time to introduce him to the people who'd become his family. "The Logans are having a barbecue on Saturday. And I'm not working. Would it be all right if I took Bobby?"

"Of course," she said. "The Logans are nice people. And I know how much they mean to you."

"Great. I'll pick him up about noon, if that's all right."

She cleared her throat. "I'll bring him to your house, if you don't mind."

Joe crossed his arms and leaned back in the red vinyl seat. So that's where she was coming from. Obviously, she still didn't want Joe at her house, still didn't want to chance him running into her dad.

Had time with his son not been at stake, Joe would have told her just what he thought of that damn suggestion to meet him. As it was, he swallowed the bitter taste in his mouth and wrote the directions to his condominium complex on a napkin.

Her keeping things a secret wasn't going to last for long. Joe wouldn't let it. One of these days he'd force the issue and insist they tell their son the truth. Tell Bobby that Joe was his father. And that, from now on, his dad was going to be a big part of his life.

Then they'd tell Thomas Reynolds.

The blustery old goat might get red in the face and cuss a blue streak, but he didn't scare Joe. Not anymore.

Joe didn't want to see Thomas Reynolds suffer a heart attack but, quite frankly, the man should have learned to control his temper and his blood pressure years ago.

Bobby was a Davenport.

And as far as Joe was concerned, Kristin's father could put *that* in his fancy pipe and smoke it.

Chapter Four

Kristin sat behind the wheel of her father's white Town Car and glanced at the directions Joe had written on a crumpled napkin.

"How long will it take to get there?" Bobby asked from the back seat.

"Just a few more minutes, I think." Kristin spotted the Playa del Sol condominiums up ahead and turned into the complex. She followed the roadway until it forked, then turned left, as Joe had instructed, and parked the car in one of the few visitor spaces she could find. "Well, this is it."

She studied the white stucco building, the red, Spanish tile roofs.

"Which one is his?" Bobby asked.

"Number 126. Will you help me look for it?"

"Okay." Bobby eagerly climbed from the car and began to scan the wrought-iron numbers on the front porches. "That one is 112. And there's 113."

They strode along the concrete walk that lined a freshly mowed carpet of grass. Kristin caught the salty scent of the ocean breeze, as she scanned the verdant grounds of the complex. Playa del Sol had been built in a Spanish style and landscaped with enough palms, tropical plants and flowers to give it a Mexican Riviera aura.

"There it is!" Bobby pointed to a unit with a red-flowered hibiscus growing near the door. "I'm going to ring the bell."

A wave of anticipation washed over Kristin, in spite of her efforts to forget what Joe had once meant to her, and she wiped her hands upon the sides of the pale yellow linen dress she wore.

Joe opened the door, a broad grin aimed at her son. Or rather, their son. "Hey, Bobby."

The boy beamed. "Hey, Joe."

When the firefighter cast his gaze on her, something zapped between them. She wasn't entirely sure what, but it shot a wave of excitement coursing through her veins, causing her heart to go topsy-turvy and her senses to reel. How could he still do that to her, after all these years?

After all the heartbreak, all the tears?

Kristin stood on the front porch, like an awkward adolescent on a first date. But this wasn't a date. Not at all. And she hated the idea that it felt even remotely like one, for more reasons than one.

She was over Joe Davenport. And she was engaged to another man. An exceptional man who would make a wonderful husband and father.

Hoping her nervousness didn't show, she mustered a smile. "Hi."

"Good morning, Kristin." His voice had grown deeper with age. Huskier. More able to strum upon her senses than it had in the past.

She tucked a strand of hair behind her ear. "Are we too early?"

"Not at all." He opened the door, allowing her and Bobby to enter. "Come on in."

Her son zipped right inside, eager to be in the fireman's home, while Kristin moved slowly. She noted the hardwood entry, the Berber carpet, the beige sectional against the east wall, the glass-top coffee table, where a TV remote and a *Sports Illustrated* rested.

"It's not much," Joe said. "But it suits me."

The living room was spacious and plain, with stark white walls—no artwork. The only notable decor item was a rectangular TV screen above the fireplace, like a painting. An elaborate stereo system—complete with surround sound, no doubt—sat near the dining area.

A sliding door led to the patio, where a red mountain bike was parked next to an elaborate gas barbecue grill.

Yet it was the deep blue waters of the bay that caught

her attention and drew her to the glass door. "What a beautiful view."

"You ought to see it at night."

She looked over her shoulder, caught his gaze. Caught the subtle implication that she might like to be here one evening. With him. And the stunning view.

They both let the comment ride off into the sunset.

"That's a cool bike," Bobby said. "I got a bike, too."

"Maybe we can take them out someday. To the park by the bay." Joe glanced at Kristin, his eyes asking her permission.

"That would be way cool," Bobby added. "Can we, Mom? Can Joe and I ride our bikes together?"

There was no reason why she should say no, but she'd never had to share her son before. She forced a smile. "We'll have to discuss it. And check our calendars."

Joe glanced at his wristwatch. "Well, I guess we'd better go."

Kristin turned toward the door, but he stopped her. "Just a minute. I'm supposed to bring wine, soda and a couple bags of chips. It's a potluck."

A potluck? Kristin wished she would have known. She felt kind of awkward going to Harry's house without taking anything special to contribute. In fact, just the thought made her feel like a party crasher. "If you would have told me sooner, I would have made a potato salad or a chocolate cake."

"Maybe next time," Joe said. Then he glanced at Bobby. "Why don't you help me carry things out to the car?"

Kristin followed them to the kitchen, where Joe reached into the pantry and pulled out two bags of chips—plain and barbecue. He handed them to Bobby.

As a woman who loved to cook, Kristin always took note of the kitchen in a house. She scanned Joe's countertops. Nothing fancy. Just a can opener and a coffeepot.

But near the sink, she spotted a silver-bangle wristwatch. It clearly wasn't something a manly fireman would wear.

Who did the watch belong to? A cleaning lady? A neighbor?

A lover?

Joe pulled open the refrigerator door. The shelves were practically empty, except for some condiments, two bottles of wine, a case of Mexican beer, and several six-packs of soda.

He withdrew a chardonnay and placed it on the counter, then removed packs of cola and root beer.

"Let me carry something." Kristin reached for the bottle of wine.

"All right." Joe grabbed the soda. "Come on. Let's go."

As they left the kitchen, Kristin took one last glance at the wristwatch.

Somehow, she'd failed to consider the fact that Joe might have a woman in his life—maybe several—and for some illogical reason, it didn't sit well with her, even though she had a fiancé of her own.

A *wonderful* fiancé, she reminded herself. A well-respected, down-to-earth doctor with a quick wit and a ready knowledge of psychology and human relation-ships. A handsome man who would be a perfect addition to her and Bobby's lives.

So why the silly fascination with Joe?

Just curiosity, she supposed, and a case of auld lang syne. Every once in a while, when she thought of some classmate she'd gone to school with, she often wondered what he or she was doing now. This was no different.

So she tried her best to disassociate herself from the past and focus on the future.

But whenever her gaze drifted to the golden-haired fireman with the glimmering amber-colored eyes and bad-boy smile, her memories came crashing back, front and center.

As they pulled in front of the Logans' two-story house on Bayside Drive, Joe parked, and they climbed from the Tahoe. Kristin continued to carry the bottle of wine, glad she could hold onto something and still sorry she hadn't baked a cake or prepared an appetizer. She made a killer artichoke dip. And her crab salad always went over well.

At the elementary school where she worked, the teachers and staff often got together and had potlucks, which helped to create a better working environment for everyone.

Next time, if she ever had the opportunity to attend another Logan party, she would definitely bring something to show her appreciation.

The Logans were practically famous for their outdoor barbecues and their hospitality. At least they had been years ago, and Kristin doubted things had changed.

A floral welcome mat awaited them on the front steps, and Joe rang the bell. Moments later, Kay Logan answered.

Harry's wife was an attractive, rosy-cheeked woman with copper-colored hair. She smiled warmly and gave Joe a big hug. "Who have you got here?"

Joe introduced the women, saying, "You may not remember, but you met once before. About eight years ago."

"Of course." The petite, older woman smiled at Kristin. "We're always glad to have the boys bring along their friends."

"It's good to see you again, Mrs. Logan. Thanks for including us."

The older woman took Kristin's hand and gave it a warm squeeze. "Please call me Kay."

Joe slipped an arm around their son's shoulder. "This is Bobby. Kristin's son."

A twinge of guilt knotted in Kristin's chest. The Logans were like family to Joe. And she knew he would have liked to have introduced Bobby as his son. But she couldn't allow the Bayside community to know something her father had yet to learn.

"I'm so glad you came, Bobby." Kay stepped aside. "Come on in."

"Where would you like the wine?" Kristin asked.

"In the fridge for now." Kay took the chips from

Bobby, then touched Joe's forearm. "Why don't you boys take the sodas outside? Harry has a tub filled with ice on the porch."

Kay led Kristin into the kitchen, a big, functional room with wallpaper trim in a violet motif. The white countertops boasted all of the appliances a woman who loved to cook and entertain would need.

"You have a lovely house," Kristin commented. "And a great kitchen."

"Thank you." Kay grinned, her cheeks blushing with pride. "I want a place my kids can call home."

As Kay put the wine in the refrigerator, Kristin glanced at the breakfast nook, a cheery sitting area with pale lavender walls and a large bay window framed by a valance of Irish lace.

The window looked out into a moderate-size yard filled with plants, ferns and palm trees—each one trimmed neatly. On the patio, a built-in barbecue grill sat amidst redwood furniture.

Joe stood next to Bobby, his hand resting proudly on his son's shoulder. The man and boy looked remarkably alike, and she wasn't so sure either Kay or Harry had failed to notice. But they hadn't said anything. And neither would she. Not until her father's health improved.

Not until the doctors felt confident enough to schedule the bypass surgery he needed.

As Harry shook Bobby's small hand, his eyes sparkled with a sincere welcome. The retired detective appeared older than Kristin remembered—a bit more gray, his receding hairline more pronounced—but he was still tall and powerfully built.

She stood like that for a while, like a voyeur, until Kay's voice drew her from the window. "You're Thomas Reynolds's daughter, aren't you?"

"Yes. I am."

"If I remember correctly, you used to date Joe. Years ago."

Kristin nodded. "Before college."

Before he grew tired of her.

"Joe was quite smitten with you," Kay said with a knowing smile.

Kristin merely returned the smile, rather than utter the first thing that came to mind.

Joe hadn't stayed smitten for long. He'd dumped her and broken her heart.

"Well," Kay said, obviously taking Kristin's silence as a hint to change the conversation to a more appropriate topic. "I doubt Joe will appreciate my rambling off like that. Can I pour you a glass of wine? Or a soda?"

"Actually, I'm fine for now. Thank you."

"Well, in that case," Kay said. "Let's go outside and join the men."

Joe watched, as Kristin stepped onto the patio. The sun glistened off the gold highlights in her honey-blond hair. She'd always been pretty. Classy. The kind of woman a man like him shouldn't even dream about having at his side.

She wore a pale yellow dress today. Linen, he guessed. Pearl earrings and a necklace reminded him that she was a lady made for a different life than he could have offered her.

And the past eight years had only made her prettier. More classy. More out of reach.

Still, just looking at her made his pulse do all kinds of crazy things.

"Kristin," he said, trying to shake off a goofy adolescent reaction. "You remember Harry Logan, don't you?"

"Yes, of course." She extended her hand. "It's good to see you again."

"This is Kristin Reynolds," Joe told the retired detective.

If Harry held any animosity toward Kristin's old man, as Joe still did, he didn't show it. "I'm glad you could join us, Kristin. Can I get you a soda? A beer? Maybe a glass of wine?"

"No, thank you," she said. "Not yet."

A doorbell sounded, followed by Nick Granger's voice. "Anybody home?"

Nick had once been a delinquent, like Joe. But, thanks to Harry, he was now a detective with the San Diego Police Department. And he was also the Logans' new son-in-law, having married Harry's daughter, Hailey.

Joe introduced Kristin to an obviously pregnant Hailey, and the women seemed to hit it off. Well, at least that's how it seemed when Kristin asked Hailey when the baby was due. Women sure seemed to get a kick out of talking about stuff like that.

Before long, the house and yard were filled with friendly faces and good-natured laughs of the guys who'd once had troubled backgrounds, like Joe's. Years ago, they'd been dubbed Logan's Heroes by the men on the police force because of Harry's interest in the angry misfits. The moniker had been made tongue in cheek, until one by one, the delinquents each turned their sorry lives around and become heroes in real life.

The guys had found a family with the Logans and had bonded with each other. There wasn't anything Joe wouldn't do for Harry, Kay or any one of the men Joe thought of as his brothers. And he knew each of them would do the same for him.

Brett Tanner, a Navy helicopter pilot, walked outside, tossing a Nerf football in his hand. "Anyone up for a game?"

"I am!" Bobby shouted.

A sense of pride settled over Joe, and he wished he could introduce the boy as his son. But he and Kristin had made a bargain, which he meant to keep—unless she failed to keep her part of the agreement.

But either way, he had big plans to play catch-up in his relationship with Bobby. And nothing would stand in his way.

Kristin laughed at something Hailey said, and Joe couldn't help but stare. Nor could he help but admire the lilt of her voice. The way she carried herself in a crowd.

"Heads up," Brett called to Joe, as Bobby's launch of the blue, lightweight ball zoomed out of bounds.

Joe snagged it in the air, then passed it right back to his son, joining in the game.

Bobby had good hands for a kid. A chip off the old block, Joe supposed, unable to wipe the sappy grin from his face.

Before long, a major Nerf Super Bowl erupted on the lawn. Laughter broke out, as the men reined in their normally competitive streaks whenever Bobby was in the play.

Several plays later, Joe noticed a big grass stain on the knee of Bobby's khaki dress slacks. Kristin, who had always dressed like a fashion plate, had transferred her taste and choice in clothing to Bobby. The poor kid looked as if he'd stepped out of a kid's wear catalogue. Too bad she couldn't let their son be a kid.

Of course, Joe didn't want to rock the boat right off, so he decided to buy some jeans, T-shirts and sneakers to keep at his house, stuff normal kids wore because playing rough and getting dirty was a given.

At least Kristin wasn't harping on the boy about staying clean and spiffy.

After a handoff to Bobby, Joe blocked Nick, allowing the boy to run up the middle and score. It always felt good to play ball with the men he thought of as brothers. But even more so to include his son in their camaraderie.

Joe glanced at Kristin, spotted her smiling at something Kay said. He hoped it wouldn't be long before she agreed to tell Bobby the truth, because he was tired of sitting on the sidelines.

Joe Davenport was ready for the world to know he had a son.

As the afternoon sun lowered in the western sky, the scent of charcoal and the aroma of burgers sizzling on the grill filled the air.

"Are you ready for something to drink now?" Kay asked Kristin, while the women sat outside on the redwood furniture.

"Sure. Wine sounds good."

"I have a merlot, the chardonnay you bought, or some white zinfandel," Kay said. "Which would you prefer?"

Kristin had taken a Wines and Foods of Italy class through the extended studies department of the college back home. And she'd grown to appreciate the taste, especially when having a special dinner. But it wasn't as though she had a real yearning to have a glass now. She would probably nurse it all afternoon. "How about the merlot?"

"You've got it." Kay turned to Hailey. "Can I get you something, too, honey? I've got milk and juice."

Hailey rubbed her pregnant tummy and smiled. "Apple or orange juice sounds good, if you have one or the other."

"I have both," Kay said proudly. "Your father loves his juice in the morning. And I know how much you enjoy it, too."

"Then make it apple," Hailey said.

Kay left the two women sitting under the shade of a maple tree in the yard.

"Your parents are really special," Kristin said.

Hailey nodded. "They are at that. My mother passed away a few years ago, but Kay has accepted me as the daughter she never had."

Kristin hadn't realized Hailey, who'd been introduced to her as the Logans' daughter, wasn't a child of their union. But she wasn't surprised. The Logans had opened their hearts and their home to a lot of people, particularly to the guys like Joe.

Harry and Kay had made a big impact on Joe's life, as well as the lives of most everyone here. And as far as Kristin was concerned, the older couple deserved a special place in heaven for their efforts.

She looked at the guys playing football with her son, knowing that they'd gone out of their way to make him feel like a part of the team—a lesson they'd no doubt learned from Harry and his wife.

And strangely enough, as the afternoon wore on, she felt as though she belonged here, too.

She'd met a lot of new faces today, including Hailey's husband Nick. She'd also been introduced to Brett Tanner, a Navy helicopter pilot, and Luke Wynters, an E.R. doctor at Oceana General Hospital. And those were just the names she could remember right off.

Surprisingly, the lazy afternoon spent with the Logans was one of the most pleasant outings she'd had in a long time. Everyone had made her feel welcome, although she still would have preferred to have placed her own homemade dish on the buffet table in the yard. But she no longer felt out of place.

Kay walked out the sliding glass door, with a full glass of apple juice in one hand and a goblet of red wine in the other. Kristin got up from her seat and met the woman halfway.

"Let me take that," Kristin said, accepting the wineglass. "Are you having something to drink?"

"Yes," Kay said. "I've got an iced tea in the kitchen."

"I'll get it for you."

"Thanks."

As Kristin made her way across the yard, one of the guys hollered, "Watch out. Don't hit Joe's lady."

Joe's lady?

That couldn't be further from the truth, yet the term slid over her like a black, slinky negligee. She glanced at Joe, wondering whether he'd set the guys straight. But he didn't say a word. And she wasn't sure whether she should be happy or annoyed.

She found Kay's iced tea on the counter, picked it up and carried it, along with her glass of wine, back outside.

From out of nowhere, a spiraling blue blur came flying toward her, followed by a shadowed hulk. Upon impact, she fell to the ground with a thud. When her head cleared and her eyes opened, she found Joe hovering over her.

"Oh, God, Kristin. I'm *so* sorry. Are you okay?"

"I think so." She held an empty wineglass in her hand. Kay's drink had slipped from her grip, shattered on the porch and sent tea, ice cubes and shards of glass across the concrete slab.

But for some reason, she couldn't seem to focus on the mess or on the awkward position she was in.

Not while Joe leaned over her, his hand on her shoulder, his eyes wide and full of remorse mingled with compassion. His sea-breezy scent taunted her senses and set off a flurry of pheromones that dazzled her and left her speechless.

"Did I hurt you?"

Not this time. But eight years ago, you knocked me for a loop and shattered my heart. She managed a smile. "I'm just a bit shaken up. And embarrassed. But I'm all right."

"I'm really sorry, Kristin." Joe took her by the hand and helped her get to her feet, then his eyes lowered.

She followed his gaze to the damp splotch on her chest, where the red wine had soaked into pale yellow linen.

Brett—or was it Luke?—came bounding toward her. "I'll get the glass picked up. But you'd better get that dress rinsed."

"It's all right," she said, although she doubted the stain would come out.

"Are you sure you're not hurt?" Joe stroked her arm, sending a shimmy of heat through her blood.

She shook off her reaction to his touch. "Don't worry about it. I'm tough. Really."

"Come on." Joe took her by the hand, his grip much larger than she remembered. Much warmer. More gentle.

"You'll find club soda in the bar," Harry said from where he stood at the grill. "That ought to get the stain out."

"I've got a product that can clean anything," Kay said, as she made her way toward the house. "Let me get it for you, as well as something to wear. You'll need to soak that dress."

Joe led Kristin into the kitchen, where he looked at her as though he'd just run over his dog. He lifted a hand to her hair, touched the strands. His fingers drifted to her cheek, as those topaz-colored eyes snagged hers. "Are you sure you're okay?"

She nodded, unable to tear her gaze from his. Their movements froze, momentarily, until he broke the visual connection and glanced down at her chest.

He touched the spot, right over her left breast, where the merlot had absorbed into the cloth, his fingers warming her to the bone.

Her heart thudded in her chest, as though intending to leap right out of her body. Could he hear the darn thing pounding? She didn't doubt it. Her pulse was thumping in her head like a runaway train.

Neither of them spoke or moved. They just stood there, caught up in something odd. Something warm and sweet, something hot and wild.

Something totally out of line.

Kristin had a fiancé, for goodness sake. A man who thought she was home taking care of her ailing father, not stirring up old memories and forbidden passion with an old lover.

She laughed and stepped back. "It's all right. Really. I can get this."

Joe opened his mouth, as though intending to speak, then snapped it shut. He nodded instead, then left her alone in the kitchen.

What was that all about? Had Joe been rattled by the touch, the intimacy? Had he felt that same sensual connection?

It would seem so.

But Kristin had no desire to strike up that kind of a relationship with her son's father. Not when Dr. Dylan Montgomery was the man in her life.

What kind of stupid was that?

Kristin was an engaged woman. A happily engaged woman. She blew out a ragged sigh and glanced down at her damp chest, where she could still feel the warmth of Joe's hand.

And where red wine marred her dress like a blazing scarlet letter.

Chapter Five

If Bobby noticed the awkward silence between the adults on the way back to Joe's condo, Kristin certainly couldn't tell by his happy chatter. He'd obviously had a great time at the barbecue.

And so had Kristin. Other than that embarrassing tumble and the sexual reaction she'd had to Joe's concern, his scent, his touch.

She studied her lap, particularly the bright floral material of the pants Kay had loaned her—pants that had been too big at the waist. Of course, a safety pin and an oversize pink T-shirt hid that.

But the pants weren't very stylish—at least, not by a younger woman's standards. And the hem hit too high above the ankles.

Of course, that didn't mean Kristin didn't appreciate Kay loaning the clothes to her so she could soak her dress in that super-duper stain remover the older woman swore by.

Kristin took a quick peek at Joe and tried to guess what he was thinking or feeling and had no luck at all. Was he bothered by the sensual connection they'd shared this afternoon?

Had it unnerved him as badly as it had her?

Or was he trying to put some distance between them, afraid that she'd think he still felt something for her when, eight years ago, he'd made it clear that he didn't.

Surely not. He knew that she had a fiancé. And she knew he had someone, too. Joe Davenport was too darn good-looking to be unattached. Besides, that silver-bangle watch sitting on his countertop certainly suggested there was a woman in his life.

"Thanks for taking me and my mom to the barbecue," Bobby said from the back seat. "It was really fun. I liked playing football with the guys."

"They liked playing with you, too, Bobby." Joe slid a glance at Kristin, but she couldn't read the expression on his face. And she was angry with herself for even trying.

There was nothing between her and her old lover. Not anymore.

At the next stoplight, Joe looked across the seat and caught her eye. "I have Tuesday off. And if you don't mind, I'd like to take Bobby on that bike ride we talked about earlier."

"That would be way cool," Bobby said. "Can I, Mom? Please?"

Kristin was hard-pressed to come up with an excuse to say no. She didn't have anything on her calendar, other than her father's appointment with the internist on Friday. That was the only day that wouldn't work this week because she planned to go, too. She needed to ask the doctor a few questions and gain a better understanding of her father's medical condition and treatment options. But Tuesday was definitely free.

She didn't dare look at Bobby, because he was probably holding his breath, waiting for her to agree. And if she stammered and flubbed up a lame excuse, Joe might think that whatever happened in Kay's kitchen had affected her more than she wanted him to suspect.

There was, she realized, no real reason to say no. "I suppose Tuesday is as good a day as any. What time would you like me to bring him over?"

Joe focused straight ahead. On the traffic? Or avoiding her gaze?

She wasn't sure, but when he did look her way, his eyes drilled right into her like sharpened topaz.

"You don't want me to come to your father's house and pick him up?"

Okay. So there it was. He suspected that she wasn't ready for him to meet her dad face-to-face.

She wanted to explain, but with Bobby hanging on to every word of their conversation, it was best to let it go. Besides, it didn't really matter anyway. She didn't intend to reveal Joe's part in Bobby's conception, but she couldn't keep the fireman's involvement with her son a secret for long.

"Maybe you *should* pick him up," Kristin said. "Bobby's bike will fit in your SUV better than in my dad's Town Car."

"Why don't I come over about ten?"

"That'll be fine."

Bobby cheered from his seat in back, then began to chatter about bikes, scooters and Rollerblades. Before long, the silver Tahoe pulled into Joe's complex, marking the end of the day.

"Thanks for taking us to the Logans with you," Kristin said. "We had a great time."

"You're welcome." Joe parked in his driveway. "I'm sorry about knocking you down and staining your dress."

"Don't worry about it." She managed a carefree smile. "Those things happen."

As they got out of the Tahoe, Kristin carried the wet dress in a plastic grocery bag. "I'll get Kay's clothing returned as soon as I can."

"Or I can take it to her," Joe said. "Whatever is easiest for you."

Before Kristin could respond, a tall, shapely redhead dressed in a black formfitting dress and spike heels waved her arm and wiggled her fingers. "Joe! You're home. I was afraid you wouldn't be here in time."

In time for what?

Kristin looked at Joe, but his smile didn't explain anything. And she'd be darned if she would ask.

"I'd never let you down," Joe told the redhead. "Chloe, I'd like you to meet my friends, Kristin and Bobby."

The redhead—Chloe—extended a hand and flashed a smile outlined by lipstick the color of pink cotton candy. "I'm glad to meet you. Joe and I are neighbors."

The busty woman's hair might have been red to begin with, but the color had definitely been enhanced by a dye job. In fact, it looked good. Remarkably good. And Chloe had to know it, because she fairly glowed with sexual confidence.

An unwelcome and unreasonable sense of jealousy bubbled under Kristin's calm surface as she greeted the woman.

Was Chloe, as she had said, just a neighbor? Was she the owner of the watch?

She certainly wasn't his cleaning lady. Not dressed like that. Did she and Joe have a date tonight? And if so, were they lovers?

Kristin tugged at the oversize shirt with Bingo Babe written across the chest, then shook the flamboyant woman's hand.

Wasn't anyone going to mention this evening and what the two *neighbors* had planned?

Kristin glanced at Joe, at that darn poker-faced expression on his face. No clue there. Not even a you-look-hot-baby glimmer in his eye when he looked at Chloe.

But how could he not notice how sexy the redhead was? She'd practically poured herself into the curve-hugging dress that could scarcely contain her breasts.

Okay. So it wasn't any of Kristin's business what was going on between Chloe and Joe. Who cared about how the handsome fireman spent his free time?

The truth settled over her like a wet blanket.

She cared.

But she shouldn't.

Of course, since Bobby was going to spend more time with his father, it really *did* matter who Joe's friends were.

Maternal interest took hold, and Kristin shook off any personal curiosity. "Thanks for taking us to the barbecue. Bobby and I are going to head home."

"Thanks for going with me." Joe gently stroked the top of Bobby's hair. "I'll see you on Tuesday, sport."

Kristin pasted what she hoped was a nondescript expression on her own face. "Goodbye. We'll see you Tuesday."

Then she led her son—*their* son—back to her father's car and headed home.

But she couldn't help a quick glance in the rearview mirror.

Nor could she ignore the twinge of jealousy that squeezed her heart, when Joe and Chloe stepped into his condo and closed the door.

On Tuesday morning, Joe loaded up his bike, then knocked on Chloe's door. Her blinds were pulled, suggesting she was asleep. But he didn't let that bother him, since they were friends. Good friends.

After he knocked, he wondered whether he should have called first. She might have had someone sleep over, even though her dates were usually limited to one or two per guy and rarely got to the let's-get-naked stage. But what the heck? Chloe probably wouldn't mind. She owed him, especially after the other night.

When she didn't answer, he rang the bell.

A minute or so later, she opened the door wearing a white, fluffy robe and looking like a long-haired Little Orphan Annie with a sleepy-eyed grimace. "Hey. What's up?"

"Rise and shine, beautiful. Shouldn't you be up by now? Isn't this the day you're supposed to work at that critter rescue place?"

"Yeah." She squinted in the sunlight and yawned. "What time is it?"

"About quarter to ten."

"I had a late night. I went out with Antoine, my hairdresser, and some of his friends." She stepped aside. "Want a cup of coffee? You'll have to make it, though. I need to jump in the shower."

"Nope. I didn't come over to chat. I just want to borrow your bike."

Chloe ran a hand through her hair, an acrylic nail snagging on a rumpled red curl. "What for? You've got a nice one of your own."

"I'm taking the kid you met the other day out for a

ride along the bay, and I thought his mom might want to join us."

Chloe's eyes widened, then she slid him a dimpled grin and crossed her arms over the white chenille that covered her breasts. "Sounds like you're *hoping* the mom will join you."

"I'm not interested in the mother."

Chloe lifted an auburn brow. "Oh no?"

"Nope."

Been there, done that. But Joe didn't mention anything to Chloe. They might be good friends, but they weren't that good. He didn't blab about stuff he'd locked deep in his gut. Not even to his closest buddies.

Joe and Chloe had actually dated once, when he first moved into Playa Del Sol. But the evening had been a disaster in a romantic sense, as he suspected most of Chloe's dates were. And it hadn't taken either of them very long to realize they had nothing in common.

Chloe was a pretty woman who tried to hide her insecurities behind a facade of spritz, spandex and makeup. But her biggest flaw was a heart as vast and deep as the Pacific. Not to mention a naiveté that was sometimes surprising in this day and age.

But she also had more underneath a flashy surface than most people realized. Chloe was a special lady, in her own, unique way.

The pretty redhead had more in common with Little Orphan Annie than hair color. And in spite of a crappy childhood, Chloe was dead set on saving the world, at least in a bless-the-beasts-and-the-children sense.

But Joe suspected the woman who had very few female friends really needed someone who would save her from herself.

"Kristin dresses a little matronly for a woman her age," Chloe said. "And the pearls didn't do a thing for me. Too Doris Day and June Cleaver."

Joe smiled. "The clothes Kristin wore the other day didn't belong to her."

"Whatever." Chloe led Joe into the darkened house and kicked aside a pair of lime-green high heels he suspected she'd worn last night and shed in the entryway when she'd returned. "It's parked on the patio."

When Joe came back inside, wheeling the bike, he found Chloe seated on the sofa, her feet tucked under her.

She opened her mouth to speak, and a yawn caught her off guard, but that didn't stop her from talking right through it. "Thanks…for taking…care of my old folks the other night."

"No problem. I actually enjoyed chatting with Mr. Johnston. He's got some interesting war stories. And a unique philosophy on life."

"Did you make sure Mrs. Irving saved her dessert for last?"

"Come on. I wasn't about to tell that ninety-six-year-old woman that she shouldn't eat her pudding first."

A grin tickled her lips. "You big softie."

"Look who's talking," he said, with a laugh. "You've

been taking meals to the seniors in this community for as long as I've known you. And then there's all that time you spend at the animal shelter, not to mention those trips to that orphanage in Baja."

"Tease me all you want," she said with a smirk. "But it looks as though you've taken on a little pet project of your own. Single moms have never been your date of choice."

"They still aren't." He glanced at his watch. "Listen, I've got to go. Thanks for letting me borrow your bike."

"No problem." Chloe continued to grin like a fat cat locked in the creamery at the dairy.

When Joe reached the front door, he paused. "You never did tell me how that date with Arturo went."

She blew out a raspberry with her tongue. "It went in the toilet. Or should I say *en el escusado?*"

That didn't surprise Joe. That's where most of Chloe's dates ended up. She always had such high hopes, but she'd never been attracted to the kind of guy she deserved. And he wasn't sure why. "Was the language a problem?"

"I know enough Spanish to get by," she said. "So while we had margaritas, we chatted. I didn't understand everything he said, but I know what a matador is. It's a bullfighter. And you know how I feel about animals."

Yeah. He knew how she felt about all living creatures. If she found a spider in her bathtub, she'd pick it up carefully in a tissue and carry it outside to set it free. "I can see where your two worlds might collide."

She shrugged her shoulders, then nibbled on an acrylic nail. "I'm not so sure that I'll ever find Mr. Right. It seems I keep running into Mr. All That's Left."

That was probably true, although he thought it was her own fault. Maybe she was only attracted to losers.

It was a shame, too. Chloe actually had a lot going for her in addition to her looks, her heart and a hefty trust fund that allowed her to not only get by without needing a regular paycheck, but to donate to the many charities she supported.

Joe had a feeling that Chloe kept setting herself up for failure. But who was he to point fingers?

He hadn't been able to find anyone to measure up to Kristin Reynolds since he let her go. And God knew she was a benchmark not many women could reach. Except maybe for Allison, a pretty flight attendant he'd been dating. But the jury was still out on that budding relationship. Their schedules didn't allow them much time together.

"Have a good day, Chloe. Maybe love will fall in your lap when you least expect it."

"Maybe so," she said. "But I'm learning not to hold my breath."

When Joe had loaded her bike onto the rack attached to his SUV, he headed toward Thomas Reynolds's house, intent on picking up his son. And if Kristin wanted to go along, he was prepared. At least as far as having wheels for her to ride.

He wasn't sure it was a good idea to encourage her

to go with them to Bayside Park. Not after they'd gotten caught up in that sensual cloud of…whatever it was.
Hell, resurrecting those old feelings for Kristin would
only complicate his life. Especially since the only thing
they had in common was Bobby.

Ten minutes later, Joe pulled into the long drive that
led to Thomas Reynolds's house. Bobby was sitting on
the front porch, his hair all combed, his freckled face
aglow with a bright-eyed smile. A new, shiny red bicy-
cle waited on the grass.

"Hey, sport. While I load your bike, why don't you
let your mother know I'm here?"

Bobby tore off like a shot. Moments later, he led his
pretty mom outside. She wore a pair of long, khaki
walking shorts and a crisp white blouse. Nothing
fancy, yet classy. And undoubtedly appropriate for a
wealthy woman.

No spritz, no spandex, no makeup to speak of, other
than rose-colored lipstick.

Yet Joe's pulse kicked up a notch when he saw her,
stirring up the old memories, the old feelings he'd
thought had been buried years ago.

How could she still do that to him when she appeared
so prim and proper?

Even as a teenager, she dressed conservatively and
hadn't worn shorts very often. Was she planning to go with
them for a bike ride? Or would she let Bobby go alone?

Joe shouldn't care. But for some reason, he did. And
in spite of his better judgment, he couldn't help think-

ing it would be nice to have Kristin along, to see her loosen up a bit. Maybe coax a smile or a laugh from her.

For Bobby's sake, of course.

He slid his son's mother an easy grin. "I borrowed Chloe's bike, just in case you'd like to ride with us."

Kristin had hoped Joe would include her. And she'd dressed accordingly. But the fact that he'd borrowed his sexy neighbor's bike was a bit unsettling. And she'd be darned if she knew why.

What did it matter if Joe and his neighbor were lovers?

She managed a smile. "I haven't ridden a bike in years, but it sounds like fun."

"Good."

Two hours later, as the sun glistened over Bayside Park and Marina, Kristin, Joe and their son rode bikes along a scenic path. They'd stopped along the way several times. To get a drink of water. To stretch their legs. To eat a hamburger at a sidewalk stand.

But this time, they stopped to rest on the grass, where they watched the antics of a couple of seagulls.

"This is the funnest day of my whole life," Bobby said, eyes gleaming.

"I'm glad." Joe looked at Kristin, then returned his focus to Bobby. "This has been a pretty special day for me, too. And if your mom doesn't mind, I'd like to spend more time with you."

"That would be way cool." Bobby cast her a pleading glance. "You don't mind, do you, Mom?"

Yes, she minded. In a way. But she wasn't about to

disappoint her son. "I'm glad that you and Joe have fun together."

Bobby glanced at the helmet in his hands, then looked up at Joe. "What kind of things did you do for fun when you were a kid?"

"I didn't get to do too much stuff when I was your age." Joe glanced at Kristin, and she suspected he was trying to tap-dance around the truth.

Joe's childhood hadn't been particularly pleasant, although she didn't know all of the details. He'd been pretty tight-lipped about his past while they were dating. But she knew his dad had been a druggie and a low-life, and she appreciated him glossing over the ugliness for Bobby's sake.

"You didn't get to play?" Bobby asked. "Not even at recess?"

"I played at school. But there wasn't much money for toys at home." Joe tapped a finger on Bobby's nose. "But don't worry about me. I've made up for that now that I'm grown up. I work hard when I'm on duty. And I play hard when I'm not."

"What do you mean? Do you have toys now?"

Joe chuckled. "Grown-up toys. Like surfboards, Jet Skis and a fancy set of golf clubs. While I'm off duty, I know how to have fun. I play a little golf with a doctor buddy of mine. And I spend a lot of time at the beach."

"I like the beach, too," Bobby said. "And I want to learn how to surf."

"If it's okay with your mom, I'll give you a few lessons."

They both looked at Kristin, and she nodded. Joe certainly meant what he said about being a part of their son's life. And she wasn't sure how she felt about it. Torn, she supposed. Yet pleased.

She couldn't help but study father and son. Couldn't help but appreciate the easy smiles and laughter that Joe coaxed from Bobby.

Spending the day together had been pleasant. Special. Heartwarming and fun.

Is this what she could expect when she and Dylan were married?

Kristin looked at the rugged fireman who sat beside her. The sun glimmered off the golden highlights in his hair. And when he caught her eye and slid her a bad-boy grin, her heart skipped a beat in a way it hadn't done in years.

No, something told her. An outing with Dylan and Bobby wouldn't be like this at all.

At the end of the day, Joe took Kristin and Bobby back to her father's house, where a black Mercedes convertible was parked in the drive. Out-of-state specialty plates reading DR DYLAN told Joe who had come to visit.

"Hey," Bobby said. "What's he doing here?"

"He's been in Los Angeles this past week, filming a television special. Apparently, he's come down to visit." Kristin's cheeks had taken on a rosy glow.

Sunburned from an afternoon by the bay? Or

flushed? Joe wasn't sure. But like Bobby, he wondered what the good ol' doctor was doing here, too.

Had Dylan Montgomery, better known as Dr. Dylan of book and TV fame, come to claim his future wife and stepson?

The thought tore at Joe's gut. It was one thing sharing his son with Kristin. And something completely different when he thought of sharing the boy with another man.

The fact that the doctor was sleeping with Kristin didn't sit too well with him, either. But he wouldn't go there. Not on a bet.

Things were over between them. And besides, an awful lot had happened in the past eight years.

The front door swung open, and a tall, dark-haired man in a snazzy three-piece suit strolled outside. He sported a fresh haircut, a mustache and a bright-eyed smile. A pair of horn-rimmed glasses gave him an air of wisdom and professionalism.

But Joe found it hard to be impressed.

The psychologist approached Kristin and took her in his arms. "Surprised to see me, honey?"

She kissed him lightly on the lips. "Yes, of course. How long can you stay?"

"A day or two."

It was a formal greeting. Uptight, actually.

Because of Joe's presence? Maybe. But Joe suspected their relationship lacked passion. Or did he only wish that were the case?

Did things heat up when they were alone? In bed?

His stomach knotted when he thought of Dylan holding Kristin in his arms, kissing her. Did she still make those little whimpering sounds right before she climaxed?

Damn. He raked his fingers through his hair, trying to rid himself of the crazy, inappropriate thoughts.

Why did the idea of their lovemaking bother him?

He wasn't sure. Maybe because this pansy of a guy was supposed to be a better match for her than he'd been. At least Dr. Dylan was a man her father approved of.

But hell, Joe had let Kristin go a long time ago, freeing her to make something of her life with someone like Dylan.

Kristin's fiancé reached out his arm to greet Joe. "Dr. Dylan Montgomery."

"Joe Davenport."

The guy's hand was pansy-soft, yet he gripped Joe in a vise-like hold, as though trying to prove himself king of the cavemen or something.

"Joe is the fireman who has taken an interest in Bobby," she said.

Oh yeah? Joe shot her a narrow-eyed glance, letting her know that he wasn't pleased about the pretense she continued to keep—especially with her fiancé. Was she trying to hide the fact that Joe had been her lover? Her *first* lover?

Their lovemaking hadn't been stiff or formal. It had been hot. Demanding. Eye-crossing and toe-curling.

"We appreciate you spending time with Bobby," the TV doctor said, flashing Joe a dazzling glimpse of his pearly white teeth. Were they expensive veneers? Or had Dylan merely been blessed with looks, personality and brains?

Either way, Joe found it hard not to be nitpicky when it came to the man who was Kristin's current lover. Did he really turn Kristin's head?

Apparently so. But that wasn't any of Joe's business. He'd walked away from their star-crossed relationship years ago—for her sake. Of course he wasn't walking away now. Not from his son.

"I'd like to see Bobby on Thursday," he told Kristin. "Maybe we'll go to the beach and give surfing a shot."

"All right." She looked at her fiancé, then at the boy who was beaming with excitement. "Bobby, why don't you take Dylan in the house."

When they were alone on the grass, Kristin chewed the last remnants of lipstick from her bottom lip, then caught Joe's gaze. "I'll tell Dylan about your relationship with Bobby this evening."

"I'd appreciate that." Joe nodded toward the house. "You don't have to come along to the beach, if that will complicate your life."

"My life is already complicated," she said.

"Mine, too. I'll see you on Thursday."

"Okay."

They stood for a moment, caught up in something weird. Something that was loaded with memories and realities too heavy to mention. A stolen kiss behind the dugout at school. A winter afternoon spent on a quilt before a flickering fire in the hearth at her dad's cabin in Julian. The day he'd broken up with her for good. The tears that slipped down her cheek. The ache in his chest that erupted into tears of his own on the walk back to his foster parents' home.

Shake it off, he told himself. A lot of time had passed. He and Kristin had different lives now, and the only thing they had in common was Bobby. Their son.

They stood there for a moment, lost in the silence of their thoughts, their memories.

Then he climbed into the Tahoe and drove away, hoping to leave the past behind him.

But those toe-curling, eye-crossing memories hovered over him and followed him all the way home. And so did the grief at what he'd let slip from his fingers.

No matter how right that decision had been.

Chapter Six

Joe finished hooking up a brand-new Nintendo Game-Cube to his television, then sat down in the leather re-cliner and took hold of the bright, purple controller.

He'd just reached the first level of Razzle-Dazzle, the latest and most popular game on the market, and hit the yellow button to make his little man jump for a sparkling diamond. When a knock sounded at the door of his condo, his thumb slipped, and the little man tumbled off a stack of barrels.

Joe's competitive streak wrestled with childish dis-appointment, but only for a moment. It was time for Kristin and Bobby to arrive, and he was eager to show his son all he'd bought.

The video game setup was just a part of the surprise. Earlier today, Joe had purchased jeans, shorts and T-shirts at a local surf shop—sharp, name-brand play clothes any Southern California kid would be proud to wear. And he'd gone grocery shopping, too. He'd picked up macaroni and cheese dinners, hot dogs, frozen pepperoni pizzas and chips. He'd gotten a couple of cases of soda pop and six different types of candy, too. Hey, who said Joe Davenport didn't know how to be a dad?

When Joe opened the door, his eyes lit on Kristin, on the perfect fit of the cream-colored slacks and sweater she wore, the glossy sheen of her hair, the sparkle in her sea-green eyes. But his smile waned when his gaze was drawn to the tall, dark-haired man who accompanied them.

What the hell was the TV shrink doing here?

Dylan Montgomery extended his hand in greeting, but this time Joe was ready for him.

"Hey, Doc." Joe gripped the pansy-soft hand in a firm squeeze. "It's good to see you again."

It wasn't, of course. But a guy had to keep up pretenses for his son's sake.

Dr. Dylan rubbed his hand, yet the smile never left his face. "It's nice of you to invite Bobby over. He really enjoys your company."

"I enjoy his company, too. He's a great kid." Joe shrugged off his critical assessment of the doctor and smiled at his son. "Hey, Bobby. I've got a surprise for you."

The boy's eyes widened and his smile brightened. "What is it?"

"I've got a new video game set up, and I want you to help me try it out."

"Cool." Bobby arched his neck, trying to see past Joe.

"Why don't you go on in and take a look," he told his son.

After the boy dashed into the living room, leaving the adults to stand awkwardly in the doorway, Joe stepped aside. "Come on in."

"No," the doctor said. "We won't intrude on your time with Bobby."

Well, then get the hell off my porch, Joe wanted to say. But he refrained from giving a snide retort. He'd managed to rein in his temper years ago. Of course, that didn't mean he didn't let it slip once in a while.

But why did he feel like letting loose now?

Dr. Dylan hadn't done anything to get him all stirred up like this—other than being the man in Kristin's life.

And so what if Kristin was going to marry the guy? It wasn't Joe's concern.

Her dad, though, was probably as happy as an over-fed Christmas goose and honking all over Bayside about his daughter's lucky catch.

Thomas Reynolds had never believed Joe would amount to a hill of garbage. The real estate baron had been wrong, of course. Joe had come a long way—although he doubted the old man would think a fireman was good enough for his daughter.

But Joe quit giving a damn about what other people thought years ago. He had his own standards to measure himself by—standards Harry Logan had modeled for him.

"Kristin and I are going to take advantage of your offer to look after Bobby," Dylan said. "We're going to spend the day visiting the museums in Balboa Park."

Wasn't that just ducky.

Joe would rather spend a lazy day at the beach. And in the past, Kristin had felt that way, too.

"There's supposed to be a great show at the Reuben H. Fleet Space Theater," Kristin added.

"Well, I won't keep you then." Joe forced a happy-go-lucky smile, as he held on to the door, ready to swing it shut.

"I…uh…hope you don't intend to let Bobby watch video games all day long," Dylan said. "Since he's an only child, he's become adept at mastering solitary play. But we'd like to see him get more fresh air and sunshine."

The TV shrink was touted to be a whiz at male-female relationships. Was he an expert on parenting, too?

Joe bit his tongue to keep from telling the doctor where to shove his child psychology books and nodded toward the living room, where Bobby sat on the floor with the GameCube controller in his hand. "Actually, Bobby and I are going to the beach. But we'll probably play Razzle-Dazzle first."

Joe would be damned if he'd let the Dr. Know-It-All order him around.

"Bobby's looking forward to surfing," Kristin said, handing Joe a blue canvas bag she'd held at her side. "Here's his swimsuit, a towel and some sunscreen."

Joe took it from her. Had her hand trembled? Or was that just his imagination?

"Please keep an eye on him," she added. "And don't let him go to the bathroom alone."

Kristin's concern for her son was kind of cute, touching actually. Joe's mother, before she died, had fussed over him like that—from what he could remember. He supposed moms were supposed to be worrywarts.

"By the way," Dylan interjected. "Bobby needs a firm hand. So be careful that you don't give in to him."

Joe felt compelled to slam a fist into the good doctor's handsome face, but he crossed his arms instead.

Still, enough was enough. It was one thing dealing with Kristin's instructions and insecurities. But he'd be damned if he'd let some psychology superstar try to tell him how to be a dad.

Bobby might need a firm hand. Heck, Joe had figured that out the first day he'd met him at the fire. But Joe Davenport would stumble and fumble through fatherhood on his own, thank you very much. And Dr. Dylan could go back to the TV studio and advise bored housewives how to put more excitement into their marriages.

"Kristin is too soft on the boy." The well-dressed psychologist slipped an arm around his fiancée's shoulders, then chuckled. "But don't worry. I'm coaching her. She'll toughen up."

Funny, but Joe hadn't noticed Kristin being too soft on Bobby. Nor had he noticed the boy being anything other than active, inquisitive and normally mischievous.

"Enjoy the museums," Joe said, eager to see them gone, ready to slam the door and shut out the couple so he could spend the day with his son.

"Watch him closely," Kristin said. "He's a good swimmer, but he's not used to the ocean."

"I've got an *in* with the lifeguards and the paramedics," Joe said. "Remember?"

Kristin shot him a maternal look of concern he hadn't seen on a woman since he'd gotten lost at the bus depot as a kid. And it damn near turned his heart inside out.

Instinctively, Joe reached up and cupped her cheek. "Don't worry about him. He'll be fine."

When he realized what he'd done, he dropped his hand. But something held them together. Something biological and instinctive, he supposed. At least, that's what he hoped was happening.

"I'm sure Bobby is in safe hands," Dylan said. "Come on, honey."

Then the snazzy doctor ushered Kristin toward the black Mercedes parked at the curb.

As the relationship expert reached to open the car door for Kristin, she looked over her shoulder at Joe— prolonging what little connection they'd had.

After playing Razzle-Dazzle for much longer than Dr. Dylan would have approved, Joe and Bobby put on their bathing suits and walked outside, where the surfboard was already secured to the rack on top of the Tahoe.

They spotted Chloe striding along the sidewalk, out of breath from her morning run.

She wore a pair of skimpy black shorts and a yellow bikini top that had its work cut out trying to contain breasts that threatened to pop out each time she sucked in air.

"Bobby, you remember my neighbor, Chloe, don't you?"

The boy nodded, his eyes fixed on the redhead's chest.

Chloe looked at the Tahoe, scanned the yard, then addressed Bobby. "Where's your mom?"

"She and her boyfriend, Dr. Dylan, went to some museums in the park. But Joe and I are gonna do something fun. We're going to the beach."

Chloe arched a brow and looked at Joe. "Dr. Dylan? That isn't the guy I saw on *Oprah,* is it?"

"Probably."

Chloe whistled. "Lucky lady. That's one heck of a good-looking man. And he's big on communication and sharing feelings—something my dates lack."

Yeah, well, Joe wasn't going to discuss how fortunate Kristin was to have landed the verbal Boy Wonder. Nor was he going to point out Chloe's loser radar.

"We'll see you later," Joe said. "Surf's up."

Chloe smiled. "Have fun, guys."

Ten minutes later, Joe and his son arrived at the beach and found a spot on the sand to unload their towels and things.

Bobby started toward the water.

"Hey, sport, not so fast." Joe pulled out the bottle of sunscreen from the canvas tote bag Kristin had packed. "We've got to slick on this stuff."

"Aw, do we have to? Mom's not even here. And she'd never even know."

"If you go home looking brighter than the flashing siren on a hook and ladder, she'll know. Besides, there's a thing called trust. We want her to know we'll honor her wishes, even when she's not around." Joe smeared the lotion over his son's small shoulders, down his chest and over his back. "Better get the face, too."

Bobby stood there, while Joe protected him from ultraviolet rays. Joe wasn't one to use that stuff himself, even though he knew the hazards of too much sun. He supposed that was a bit of the rebel left in him.

Or maybe it was not having anyone ever fuss over him, not having someone who loved him and depended upon him to make him consider taking better care of himself.

Nevertheless, Joe intended to look out for his son's health and safety.

"How come moms get so weird about things like using sunscreen, eating vegetables, brushing teeth and not drinking soda for breakfast, except when you've been puking all night?"

"Isn't it nice to know someone loves you?"

"I guess," Bobby said. "Did your mom make you wear a jacket when none of the other kids had to and stuff like that?"

"My mom died when I was six," Joe said. "But when she was alive, she worried about me, too."

Bobby dug his toe into the sand, then glanced up at Joe. "It's sad—your mom dying and all. It's kind of like me not having a dad."

The boy's words sliced into Joe's heart. He wanted to tell his son the truth. That Bobby *did* have a dad. That his father just hadn't known about him before. But now that he did know, he'd be a part of Bobby's life forever.

But reality stepped in. Joe couldn't say squat about Bobby's dad until Kristin gave him the okay.

"I got a grandpa, though." Bobby's face brightened.

"That's good," Joe said, unable to mask his lack of enthusiasm.

"He's really cool."

"I'll bet." Joe couldn't imagine Thomas Reynolds being anything other than a powerful man willing to bowl down anyone in his way, even a kid.

"Sometimes we go fishing," Bobby said. "And he takes me to movies. And when my mom won't let me stay up past nine o'clock, and me and my grandpa are watching TV, he'll tell her she's not being fair by making me go to bed before the show is even over."

"Is that right?"

"Uh-huh. And that's not all. He's teaching me how to play chess, too."

"That's great. I'm glad your grandfather is good to you."

And that was a fact. It didn't make Joe change his

opinion of the man, but at least the old bastard treated Bobby well.

A cynical smile tugged at his lips. But how would Thomas Reynolds feel when he learned that his beloved grandson was a Davenport—that he shared the same blood as a drug dealer and an arsonist?

Joe's smile righted itself as a problem surfaced.

When the truth was revealed, would Thomas Reynolds turn on the boy?

Two hours later, after Bobby had surfed long enough to gain an appreciation for the sport and a desire to improve, Joe and his son sat on the sand, enjoying a milkshake they'd purchased at the Beachcomber, a seaside grass shack that sold fast food and snacks.

"Do you want to eat here? Or should we pick up tacos on the way home?"

"I really like tacos," Bobby said. "But without cheese. And no hot sauce, either."

Before Joe could respond, his cell phone rang, and he answered. It was Allison, the flight attendant he'd been dating. She was calling from a layover in Honolulu.

"How have you been?" she asked.

Joe looked at his son and smiled. "Fine."

"Are you missing me yet?"

Joe hated those kinds of questions. Especially with an audience. "How was your flight to Sydney?"

"Relatively smooth and uneventful. Hey, did I happen to leave my watch at your house?"

"Yeah. In the kitchen."

"I feel undressed without it, so I had to buy another one at the airport. I can't believe that I forgot to put it on before I left your house."

Joe smiled. "You were in a hurry to get to the airport. Remember?"

She laughed. "And we spent too much time in the shower."

Yeah, he remembered. He'd had to rush to work, too.

"I'll be home again on Saturday," she said. "I'll have to come by and pick it up."

"Sure." Joe glanced at Bobby, saw him use the straw to spoon out his shake. Watched as a dollop of chocolate ran down his chin.

The boy smiled, and Joe swiped at the dribble with his finger. "You missed, sport."

"Who are you talking to?" Allison asked.

"My…" Joe paused. He'd wanted to say his son, but caught himself. "My friend. His name is Bobby, and he's seven years old."

The boy grinned, as though the friendship meant as much to him as it did to Joe.

"Well, maybe I can meet Bobby when I see you Saturday."

"Maybe," Joe said, although he wasn't so sure he wanted to add a woman to the mix—at this point.

"Well, I'd better go," she said. "I'll talk to you later."

"Yeah. Take care."

When Joe ended the call, Bobby asked, "Who was that?"

"My…" Again he paused. His lover? His girlfriend? Heck, the relationship hadn't developed enough to know exactly who Allison was. "That was just my friend."

Joe was sure gaining a lot of *friends* since Kristin re-entered his life. But he was especially uncomfortable referring to his son that way.

Life would certainly be a lot easier to deal with when Kristin allowed their secret to be told.

Or would it?

Maybe things would just get stickier, and Bobby's questions harder to answer.

Late that afternoon, Joe and Bobby returned to his condominium complex, where they spotted Chloe carrying a brown bag of groceries in her arms.

"There's your friend." Bobby pointed toward the redhead, then waved.

Chloe juggled the bag to free a hand and wiggled her fingers at the boy. A smile lit her face.

"She sure is pretty," Bobby told Joe.

"You think so?"

The boy nodded. "Is she your girlfriend?"

"Nope. Just my friend. And my neighbor."

"Do you have a girlfriend?"

Maybe. But Joe didn't want to talk to his son about Allison. "Why do you ask?"

Bobby shrugged. "I don't know. Just wondering."

"You think I need a girlfriend?"

The boy again looked at the redhead and watched as she reached her porch, shifted the grocery bag and fiddled with the key, trying to unlock her front door. "Chloe sure is beautiful."

"Yeah. I think so, too."

"And she sure has big…you know whats."

It didn't take a Rhodes scholar to figure out what the kid was looking at. Had Joe been that young when he'd first recognized a womanly shape? Of course, the way Chloe dressed didn't leave much to the imagination.

Joe's first thought was to agree with the boy's assessment and utter, "You can say *that* again." But he put a damper on the shallow male thoughts and comments, deciding to respond in a way Harry would, if the older man were sitting here.

"A woman's prettiest and most attractive feature is her heart, Bobby. And, that being the case, Chloe is just about the most beautiful woman I've ever seen."

"My mom has a big heart," Bobby said.

"Your mom is another beautiful lady." Joe parked the Tahoe, then handed the bag of tacos to Bobby. "You carry these into the house while I take the board and the other stuff."

Fifteen minutes later, after quick showers, they ate tacos and sipped sodas while seated on the floor, in front of the coffee table.

"Are you up for another game of Razzle-Dazzle?" Joe asked.

"I sure am. And I'm going to beat you, this time."

"Good luck, sport. I don't like to lose, so you'd better watch out."

They'd only played about ten minutes, which was long enough to see that the boy had inherited his dad's competitive spirit. Just as Joe's little orange man toppled in an attempt to snatch a golden ring that would take him to a higher level, the doorbell rang.

Joe handed the controller to Bobby, then answered the door. As he suspected, the cultural duo had returned. His heart did a somersault when he spotted Kristin on the porch, a smile lighting her eyes. Yet when he forced his gaze to the man at her side, he felt like blowing out a raspberry.

Shaking off both inappropriate reactions, Joe invited Kristin and her fiancé inside. "Hey, Bobby, look who's here."

While Kristin greeted her son—*their* son—Dr. Dylan asked, "How'd it go?"

"Great," Joe said. "We had a good time."

Hell, the kid could have tied Joe to a chair, set fire to the sofa and invited the neighbors in for a marshmallow roast, and Joe would have had the same answer for the annoying shrink.

"Mom," Bobby said. "Do I have to go now?"

Joe understood the boy's sentiment. Heck, he felt like chiming in, too. It was too soon for their time to be over.

"You've had all afternoon to play," Kristin said. "Thank Joe for having you."

"But we just started a game. Can't you watch us for a while?"

"I'm afraid it's time to go." She looked at Joe, as though he was supposed to help her convince the child that the visit was over.

But she was out of luck. Heck, Joe felt like digging in his heels, too. She'd had the boy for seven years, and he was just now getting a chance to know him. To love him. To bond.

How could paternal feelings develop like that—practically overnight?

Joe probably ought to feel grateful for the time they'd had together, but he still felt cheated.

How the hell was this bicoastal parenting thing going to work?

Would he get Bobby during summer vacations?

Dylan slipped an arm around Kristin and pulled her close.

Another stab of jealousy pierced Joe's chest, this one more powerful than the last. He tossed around the idea that it bothered him to see Kristin with Dylan. But only momentarily. It wouldn't do him a bit of good to contemplate a decision he'd made years ago. A decision that had been right.

And even though Joe didn't like Kristin's fiancé, that didn't mean the guy wasn't good for her. Heck, even Chloe had called Kristin a lucky girl.

So Joe focused on the resentment he felt at handing over his son to another man.

Giving up Bobby to go with his mom was one thing. But seeing him climb into that black Mercedes with the King of Psychobabble was another.

"You see what I mean?" Dylan elbowed Joe. "She's entirely too easy on the boy. And she's got to learn how to set some boundaries."

Then the psychologist strode toward Bobby. "You heard your mother, son."

The muscles in Joe's body tensed, as he watched Dylan step up to the plate. A fierce urge to protect his son washed over him. If that guy got physical with Bobby, Joe wouldn't stand by idly.

But he didn't have to do or say anything.

Bobby set down the controller and stood up. "Thanks for letting me go with you, Joe."

"Anytime." Joe still found himself wanting to clobber the psychologist for taking on a paternal role with Bobby. But he kept his mouth shut.

For now.

But the day would come when Joe would set some boundaries of his own.

With Bobby now in tow, Dylan joined Kristin at the porch and, again, slipped his arm around her, pulling her close.

Joe could have sworn he saw her grimace at the man's touch.

Were there problems in premarital heaven?

Kristin felt awkward with Dylan's arm around her, particularly with Joe looking on.

Of course, that was silly—really. And she wasn't sure why she let it bother her. After all, she and Joe had broken up years ago.

Still, she pulled free of Dylan's hold and reached out a hand to Joe. "Thanks for looking after Bobby."

Joe wrapped her fingers in his and held on a bit longer than was necessary. Or was that only her imagination? Her memories playing havoc with reality?

"Don't thank me," he said. "I plan to be a big part of Bobby's life. Remember?"

How could she forget?

And how could she ignore the crazy, unexpected feelings in her chest. Her heart had swelled and filled with warmth, which wasn't so bad. But it also thumped and bumped unpredictably, like a fumbled football bouncing out of bounds.

She wasn't at all sure how Joe's involvement in her son's life would play out. Or how she felt about his involvement in her own life.

"Well, we need to go," Dylan said, reminding her that a lot of time had passed, that the future was full of other people to consider—not just Bobby and themselves. There were Dylan's feelings to think about. And her father's.

After goodbyes were said, Dylan led them out to the street, where he'd parked.

"Joe is the neatest guy in the whole world," Bobby said, as he climbed into the back seat of Dylan's car.

Kristin glanced at her fiancé and caught a glimpse of his stoic face, as he opened the door for her.

Had Bobby's comment bothered him?

Surely not. Dylan, of all people, ought to understand a child's enthusiasm, particularly when someone had done something nice.

As the Mercedes pulled away, the adults remained quiet, lost in their thoughts, it seemed.

But Bobby continued to chatter about all the things he'd done with Joe.

"We played Razzle-Dazzle. And then we went to the beach. You should see me stand up on the surfboard." He paused momentarily. "Well, I didn't exactly stand all by myself, but almost. And Joe said I was really good for a boy my age."

Kristin smiled. "I'm sorry I missed it."

"Then we had milkshakes, and it didn't even ruin my appetite. I still ate a taco, except for the shell."

"I'm glad you had fun with Joe," Kristin said. And she meant it, even if she didn't approve of milkshakes before dinner.

"And we saw his neighbor."

"You mean Chloe?"

"Yeah, the one with the big…"

Kristin looked over her shoulder to see Bobby cupping his hands in front of his chest.

"…the big heart."

Kristin arched a brow, but didn't respond. In part, because she wasn't sure what to say. Sometimes, when Dylan was in the car, she felt as though she was a college freshman sitting in the front row of the classroom with her hand up, just waiting for the professor to shoot down her comment.

Dylan being an expert on most things wasn't a bad thing, of course. It just made it difficult sometimes.

"And Chloe's got a *super* big heart," Bobby continued. "You can practically see it jumping out of her chest. Joe said that's why she's so pretty."

"He did?" Kristin and Joe were going to have to chat about a few things. And his pretty neighbor and her big…uh-hum…heart…was one of them.

"Yep, and Joe said you've got a big heart, too. Maybe not as big as Chloe's, Mom. But you're pretty, too."

This time, Dylan glanced across the seat and caught Kristin's eye. He didn't smile.

Obviously he had some concerns about the discussion Bobby and his father had about cleavage. Or was it something else?

Surely, there was more to Bobby's rendition than met the ear. And an odd sense of curiosity niggled at Kristin more than she cared to admit.

Joe said she was pretty?

Chapter Seven

Joe had hoped Kristin would contact him so they could talk about another visit with Bobby, but she hadn't. He'd let it go for a couple days, knowing her fiancé was in town. But he wasn't going to sit on his hands any longer.

Of course, he still planned to adhere to the bargain they'd made, but since Kristin would take Bobby back to the east coast before school started, his time with his son was limited. And for that reason, Joe decided to make the first move.

He wasn't sure what her calendar looked like or if Dr. Dylan had gone back to TV-Talk-Show Land, but he was determined to schedule another outing. He picked up the phone and dialed the number she'd given him, which he assumed was the second line at the house—the only one he was allowed to call.

Maybe he could take Bobby to that new pizza place for dinner and see a movie—something appropriate for a kid. Or, if Kristin would let him keep the boy overnight, they could pitch a tent and camp at the beach.

After three rings, Joe began to think Kristin wasn't home, until a click sounded and someone fumbled with the phone. The maid or housekeeper, maybe?

But there was no mistaking the deep, baritone voice of Thomas Reynolds, as he barked out, "Hello."

"Is Kristin there?"

"No. She's gone to the market. Can I ask who's calling?"

"This is Joe Davenport."

In the following silence, the seconds ticked in Joe's head. About the time he wondered whether the line had gone dead, Reynolds finally responded. "What do you want to talk to my daughter about? I thought we'd gotten a few things straight years ago."

Joe had a compulsion to tell the man to go to hell. But he didn't. They *had* straightened things out eight years ago, when Kristin's father had come looking for Joe at the foster home in which he'd lived.

The arrogant businessman had offered Joe five thousand dollars to stay away from Kristin.

"That's more cash than you'll earn in a year working part-time at the car wash," her father had reminded him.

And it had been. That kind of money would have

made working his way through school a lot easier, but Joe Davenport couldn't be bought. And he wasn't about to give up Kristin for anything or anyone. She'd been the best thing that had ever happened to him back then. And he'd loved her.

Much to the old man's chagrin, Joe had refused the financial offer.

Reynolds had grown red in the face and bellowed out a threat to pull strings and make sure Joe ended up doing the time he should have spent when he'd burned down that neglected warehouse.

But the angry threat hadn't made Joe flinch.

Sure, the thought of going to a juvenile detention facility had been a little unnerving, but the man's temper hadn't bothered Joe a bit.

Hell, he'd learned to stand tall during his own father's drug-induced rages without caving in. And even as irate as Thomas Reynolds had been, he couldn't hold a candle to Frank Davenport—not when it came to cursing, a red-eyed glare and a stone-cold fist.

But Kristin's dad had used an unexpected weapon when he pelted Joe with the truth.

My daughter is an honor student and college-bound, but her grades have slacked and she's ready to throw it all away.

Kristin had been one of the brightest girls in school. And she'd had the world at her fingertips. Joe hadn't known she'd let her grades slip while they were dating. He'd struggled to work at the car wash in Bayside and maintain a decent GPA, since he had no other way to attend college and support himself.

My daughter never lied to me before, never snuck around behind my back. And now look at her.

Joe hadn't known that Kristin had deceived her dad, nor had he known that she had to sneak out of the house in order to see him.

Do you want to drag her down to your old man's level?

That was the last thing Joe had wanted to do. Hell, he'd been trying his best to break free of his old man's sleazy shadow as it was.

My daughter deserves someone better than the son of a convicted drug dealer who won't amount to anything. You don't have a pot to pee in or a window to throw it out of.

And Thomas Reynolds had been right. Pretty Kristin had deserved more than what Joe could offer her.

Back then.

And maybe even now.

But Bobby was another story.

"I'm not sure if Kristin mentioned it," Joe told Reynolds, "but your grandson was responsible for that fire in the lot near your house."

The old man snorted. "I heard about it. And I suppose, under the circumstances, it makes you feel good to think Bobby set a fire. But it wasn't deliberate. Not like a case of arson that burned down my warehouse and threatened an entire city block. Your teenage prank cost me nearly a hundred thousand dollars."

That was a line of bull. The fire, although a huge mistake on Joe's part, hadn't been a prank. And the insurance company had paid the damages.

Of course, it *had* cost Thomas Reynolds plenty—if the nasty blemish on his reputation as a conscientious property owner and businessman counted.

Joe tensed his jaw and bit back the words he wanted to throw at Kristin's father. If the hardened older man had gotten his way, Joe would have spent the bulk of his teen years in a juvenile work camp.

During the court hearing, Reynolds had referred to Joe with disdain, calling him, "That Davenport kid."

How would the old man react when he learned that the grandson he'd bounced upon his knee and taught to play chess was a chip off the old Davenport block?

A rebellious sense of pleasure tickled at Joe's lips, but he remembered the promise he'd made Kristin—an agreement he meant to keep, in spite of his rising temper. "I'm sorry for setting that fire and the trouble it caused you, Mr. Reynolds. But believe it or not, it wasn't an attempt to burn down your building."

As a desperate fourteen-year-old, Joe had made what he thought was a last-ditch effort to get his dad to quit dealing drugs and enter rehab. Harry and the attorney friend he'd asked to defend Joe had brought that up in court. But apparently, Thomas Reynolds hadn't accepted the excuse.

"Humph. I imagine your old man wasn't too pleased with the attention that damned fire rained down on him, either. How's he doing these days?"

Joe knew what Reynolds was up to. He was reminding Joe of his low-life roots.

"My father's dead," Joe said, although he could have added that his old man died in a prison fight five years ago. But he kept that to himself. Kristin's old man probably knew how Frank Davenport lost his sorry life; it was in the newspaper.

And if he didn't?

Then Thomas Reynolds didn't need any more ammo in his war with the Davenports.

"That's a shame," Reynolds said without any sign of emotion.

Joe shook off the older man's false sentiment and fought the compulsion to defend himself against the charges one more time. To say that he was a firefighter, a homeowner and a contributing member of the community.

Hell, he could even point out that he'd received a commendation for bravery in the line of duty last year by risking his life when he entered a burning apartment and rescued a young mother and her newborn baby.

But what was the point?

When Thomas Reynolds looked at Joe Davenport, he only saw an angry delinquent, a teenager who'd caused him a great deal of embarrassment and trouble. A kid he was still trying to get back at.

Joe changed the subject. "I've talked to Bobby about the dangers of playing with fire."

"No need to bother. I'll take care of getting that message across to my grandson." The old man cleared his throat. "I hope your chat with my daughter has nothing to do with trying to stir up an old teenage infatuation. She's engaged and looking forward to a respectable marriage with a world-renowned doctor who can offer her a bright, trouble-free future. I'd hate to think you might try to put a damper on her happiness."

"I wouldn't think of it. Just tell Kristin I called."

"Sure." The cool, curt tone of the old man's voice indicated he hadn't really heard a word Joe said. Nor had his disdain eased in the past eight years. "What's this regarding?"

Joe had half a notion to make a retort, to set Reynolds straight. But before he could open his mouth for any kind of response, a hacking cough sounded over the telephone line, making it hard for the old man to catch his breath.

"Are you okay?"

"I'm…" Reynolds wheezed, sputtered and coughed again. "I'm fine."

Joe kept his mouth shut—hard as it was—and kept his promise to keep Kristin's secret until Thomas Reynolds had bypass surgery.

"Please have Kristin call me," Joe said. Then realizing the old man might conveniently forget to pass on the message, he added, "On second thought, I'll just call back later."

"No need for that. I'll tell her." Then Kristin's old man hung up.

Joe held the receiver in his hand, long after the line disconnected.

Surprisingly enough, Kristin *did* return his call—about ten minutes later.

"What's up?" she asked.

"We need to talk. About Bobby. And other things."

"I know." She paused momentarily.

"And we need to talk in person," Joe added.

"You're right. There are a few things I'd like to discuss, too."

He wasn't about to be put off any longer than necessary. "When? Today?"

Again, she paused. "Yes. I can come by your place now, if you'll give me time to put my groceries away."

"You got it." Joe hung up the phone, ready to tackle all kinds of things—like regular visits with his son. And a biological dad's role in a child's life. And having Kristin tell Dr. Know-It-All to back off when it came to dispensing unwelcome parental advice.

Then, when it was all said and done, they could discuss telling Thomas Reynolds he'd better get used to having a Davenport in his family.

Make that two, since Joe was determined to stay involved in his son's life.

When Kristin returned from the bedroom, where she'd placed the call to Joe, her father looked up from his spot next to Bobby on the living room sofa. A cartoon movie entertained the child, but her father's interest was obviously in the conversation she'd had with the fireman.

His gaze drifted to the purse she carried. "Where are you going?"

If she told him she was on her way to see Joe, she'd get an argument—one that could send the poor man's blood pressure skyrocketing.

She hated to lie. *Again.* But what choice did she have?

That darn phone call from Joe had set off her dad and reddened his face. His blood pressure had probably reached the boiling point, in spite of the medication the doctor had prescribed to bring it down.

"I've decided to buy a new dress," she said. "Something to surprise Dylan."

Earlier that morning, her fiancé had driven back to Los Angeles to tape another session of the program he hoped would be a spin-off to his own talk show. And when he returned, if all went well, they planned to go out on the town.

"Do you need some money? Maybe a credit card?" Her dad was so generous, so thoughtful. So undeserving of her dishonesty.

Kristin smiled, trying to dislodge the guilt that nested in her chest and made it difficult to breathe, to speak. To perpetuate the lie. "I have plenty of money. But thanks for offering. Do you want me to pick out something for you? Maybe a new tie to go with that gray suit? If Dylan closes the deal on his own TV show, he'll want to host a dinner party in celebration."

Her father grinned, undoubtedly proud of her fiancé's success. "Look for a tie with a bit of yellow in it."

"I'll keep my eyes open." She kissed her son on the cheek. "Mrs. Davies said we're having chocolate pudding for dessert."

Her father humphed. "That's not pudding. It's brown gruel from that damned no-fat/no-taste cookbook she found at a garage sale."

"Can I have ice cream instead?" Bobby asked. "I don't think I'll like the pudding, if Grandpa doesn't."

Her father chuckled. "You can have a hot fudge sundae, if you'll let me have a bite."

Her father loved to eat all the wrong foods. And she suspected he still smoked. He'd always enjoyed those expensive Cuban cigars. But it was difficult to argue with a man who'd been used to the finer things in life, a man who didn't like to be told what to do.

"We'll talk about dessert later," Kristin said, as she turned and walked away.

But a cloud of guilt settled over her, as the lie followed her out the door, into the car and onto the city streets.

How she wanted to come clean, to tell her dad the truth. But his health was at stake. And even though she'd grown stronger and more independent than she'd been as a teen, she couldn't possibly tell him about Joe now. If he suffered a heart attack before the doctors could perform the bypass surgery, she'd never forgive herself.

Thomas Reynolds might be a tough businessman and negotiator—she'd heard the rumors—but he was a loving father and grandfather. And she couldn't even comprehend what life would be like without him.

Or how Bobby would take the news. He adored his grandpa.

She blew out a sigh, then tucked a strand of hair behind her ear. She'd never understood her father's inability to give Joe a chance. Nor had she understood the resentment he'd held.

Eight years ago, Joe had been a bright young man, with a fierce pride, stubborn determination and a tender heart he'd tried desperately to hide—traits that had caused Kristin to fall deeply in love with him.

Why hadn't her father been able to see the same things in Joe that she and Harry Logan had seen?

"That Davenport kid will never amount to anything," her father had told her many times, in spite of her arguments.

Kristin had always been her father's pride and joy, and she'd never seen him so angry, so demanding. But his words had fallen on deaf, love-struck ears, and she continued to see Joe on the sly—a secret she kept from Joe because his sense of honor wouldn't have allowed him to be a part of her deception.

One day, when Kristin had been feeling especially remorseful about her deceit, she'd tried to talk to her father again—to no avail.

"That Davenport kid only wants to score with you so he can get back at me for challenging that bleeding-heart cop and trying to keep a juvenile delinquent off the street." Her father's eyes had narrowed. "Maybe it's time I had a talk with that boy."

Kristin had quickly promised not to see Joe again, and her father had backed down—thank goodness—and agreed to let the subject drop.

But her promise had lasted only a week. And in spite of what it might do to her relationship with her father, she'd continued to date the young man she loved—at any cost.

One cool, crisp day during spring vacation, while Kristin was supposed to be shopping with a friend, she talked Joe into driving her out to the mountain cabin in Julian. There, she offered him her heart, as well as her virginity.

The day had been special, and the memory would stay in her heart forever. The candles she'd lit. The fire Joe had built in the hearth. The sweet love they'd made.

If she closed her eyes, she could still catch the musky scent of his cologne, still feel the heat of his kiss. Still hear the sound of their hearts beating.

Always an optimist, she'd believed her father would eventually see what she saw in Joe and accept him and their relationship, a union Kristin believed would last a lifetime.

Of course, she'd been wrong. Her father hadn't changed his mind. And in fact, he'd been right. Joe hadn't really loved her. And that was something she'd never quite gotten over.

But together, they'd conceived a child. A little boy who was more like Joe than she could have ever believed. And it was obvious that Joe cared about his son.

Kristin just hoped he wouldn't try to force her hand, try to convince her to tell her father the truth.

Not now.

Not until she knew her dad's health could take the jolt.

But deep inside, where her conscience feared to tread, Kristin wondered which would be the biggest blow to her father—the news that Joe Davenport had fathered Bobby, or learning of his daughter's deceit.

Joe paced back and forth in the living room, waiting for Kristin to arrive. They had a lot to talk about, he supposed. But as long as he focused on Bobby, on what was best for their son, he didn't expect her to fight him on liberal visitation and joint custody.

He probably ought to offer her something to drink when she got here. He had soda and beer in the fridge. And since Allison was due back in town today, he'd picked up a pack of wine coolers. The flight attendant liked those sweet, tropical drinks, but Joe couldn't stomach them.

When a light rap sounded at his door, he answered, finding Kristin on the porch, the afternoon sunshine glistening on the gold strands in her hair. She'd dressed casually—for her—in a pair of black slacks and a white cotton blouse.

She smiled, almost shyly, and he had the urge to give her a hug, to tell her they'd work things out. But he kept his hands to himself. Just seeing her turned him inside out. And something told him that touching Kristin again might set off those old feelings. Which meant he sure as hell shouldn't be gawking at her.

"Come on in," he said, regrouping.

She entered the room, bringing in a soft, feathery scent of jasmine that hadn't been in his house before.

"Can I get you something to drink?"

"Yes. Do you have any wine?"

Joe didn't keep the stuff on hand, not since he'd dated Suzanne, who'd favored merlot. "How about a wine cooler?"

"All right." Kristin followed him into the kitchen, her scent taunting him, her presence unsettling him more than he cared to admit. And he wasn't sure why.

He pulled out a beer for himself and set it on the counter, next to Allison's watch. He hadn't considered the flight attendant stopping by while Kristin was still here. Not that it mattered, he supposed, but it would be awkward having an old lover meet the new one.

And besides, he had enough to discuss with Kristin without tossing Allison into the mix.

After taking a glass from the cupboard and filling it with ice cubes, Joe popped the lid of the cooler and poured Kristin's drink. As he turned to hand it to her, he noticed her studying the watch.

Should he comment, or let it pass?

She didn't say a word, so he let it drop. After all, he'd never been one to discuss his relationships with anyone. And he sure didn't intend to start now.

When Joe handed Kristin the glass, their fingers

brushed against each other's, setting off a shimmy of warmth in his blood and a jolt to that place in his heart where old memories were stored.

Had she felt anything? He doubted it, since she carried her drink into the living room, then sat primly on the sofa.

Her cheeks seemed flushed, though. A coincidence?

"I…uh…" She bit her bottom lip and looked at him as though she didn't know what to say. "I have to tell you something."

"What's that?"

"I'm not comfortable with Bobby being around your…uh…neighbor."

"Chloe?"

"He made a comment about her…cleavage."

"Oh, yeah." Joe chuckled and settled back into his seat.

Kristin sat up straight. Didn't Joe find it inappropriate to have a discussion about women's breasts with his son? "What's so funny?"

"Bobby's a bit young to notice those things, I suppose. And Chloe does have an R-rated wardrobe. But she's a nice person."

She cleared her throat. "Bobby thinks that she has a big heart, and that's why her breasts are so large. In fact, he seems to have gotten that idea from you."

Joe looked at her as though she'd socked him in the gut. Then he sobered and pasted a smirk on his face. "So you've got it all figured out. Okay, I'll come clean about what really went on that day. Bobby and I knocked back

a couple of beers, then sat around the pool, smoking cig-
arettes and waiting for some woman with big knockers
to show up."

Her mouth dropped, and she caught his eye. When
he crossed his arms and slid her a look of annoyance,
she realized she'd offended him.

He clicked his tongue. "Come on, Kristin. Give me
credit for being more considerate than that. I want my
son to grow up to be the kind of guy who respects
women. I'm not sure what he told you, or whether he
misunderstood the conversation."

"I'm sorry. It's just that I…"

"That you what?"

"I don't know. You're a bachelor, I guess."

He lifted a brow. "And?"

"I noticed that watch on the counter. I know you've
got women who come here. And I'm concerned about
the kind of environment Bobby will be exposed to."

"Let's get something straight. Chloe is my neighbor.
That's all. We're friends. We've never slept together.
And never will." Joe set his beer on the coffee table and
stood up. He turned toward Kristin. "And in spite of having a figure that would knock most men for a loop,
Chloe isn't the shallow bimbo that she appears to be.
She's got a big heart—which, by the way, is what I
pointed out to Bobby when he brought up her physical
attributes. We discussed how a man needs to assess a
woman's beauty."

The words Bobby had uttered began to make sense,

and guilt cloaked her shoulders. She'd come to the kind of conclusion her dad might have made had he overheard Bobby's comment.

Kristin had no problem admitting when she was wrong. She set down her drink and stood. "I'm really sorry, Joe. I had no business taking offense until I'd discussed it with you first. This shared parenting is new for me."

He blew out a ragged sigh. "Yeah. It's new for me, too."

For the past seven years, Kristin had made each and every decision regarding Bobby's upbringing. And that would no longer be the case.

"Can we start over?" she asked, her eyes searching his.

He nodded, then reached out a hand, as if to shake on it, but when their fingers touched, something passed between them. Something old and heart-stirring, like a yellowed photograph. Something new and blood-pumping, like a glimpse into a crystal ball.

Their movements froze, and they merely stood there, gripped by the past, touched by the future. Caught up in something warm and powerful, something hot and wild.

Something Kristin had no business feeling.

A hundred memories swirled in her mind. The day they'd met at the high school baseball field that warm, spring afternoon. A teenage, golden-haired Adonis and his awkward attempts to make her smile. The kiss they'd shared behind the dugout, where no one could see—a sweet, shy kiss that had turned their young lives on end.

Joe's eyes darkened, and she suspected he was re-

NO POSTAGE
NECESSARY
IF MAILED
IN THE
UNITED STATES

BUSINESS REPLY MAIL
FIRST-CLASS MAIL   PERMIT NO. 717-003   BUFFALO, NY

POSTAGE WILL BE PAID BY ADDRESSEE

SILHOUETTE READER SERVICE
3010 WALDEN AVE
PO BOX 1867
BUFFALO NY 14240-9952

If offer card is missing write to: Silhouette Reader Service, 3010 Walden Ave., P.O. Box 1867, Buffalo NY 14240-1867

Do You Have the LUCKY KEY?

PLAY THE *Lucky Key Game*

and you can get

FREE BOOKS *and a* FREE GIFT!

Scratch the gold areas with a coin. Then check below to see the books and gift you can get!

YES! I have scratched off the gold areas. Please send me the 2 FREE BOOKS and GIFT for which I qualify. I understand I am under no obligation to purchase any books, as explained on the back of this card.

335 SDL D39V   235 SDL D4AD

FIRST NAME	LAST NAME

ADDRESS

APT.#	CITY

STATE/PROV.	ZIP/POSTAL CODE

🔑🔑🔑🔑 2 free books plus a free gift   🔑🔑 1 free book

🔑🔑🔑 2 free books   🔑 Try Again!

membering, too. Were his memories just as special, just as strong as hers?

He tugged on her hand and drew her closer to him, close enough to be snared by his sea-breezy scent, his topaz-colored eyes. Her heart began to race, and she licked her lips. But she didn't pull away. Didn't put a stop to whatever had set her heart racing and made her knees wobble.

She wanted to prolong that sweet, innocent memory of first love once again—if only for a moment.

Joe didn't know what had come over him, and he damn sure didn't know why he did it, but he pulled Kristin into his arms and lowered his mouth to hers.

It was crazy. Foolish. And he expected her to fight him off, to tell him no. To be offended. But she leaned into the embrace and kissed him back.

And when she parted her lips, allowing his tongue to enter the wet, velvety softness of her mouth, he was lost in a haze of passion and urges that were stronger and more grown-up than the innocent, youthful ones in the past.

She still favored spearmint breath mints, and he couldn't seem to get his fill of her taste, of her touch.

Their tongues mated in a deep, vigorous hunger that couldn't be sated. Hell, that shouldn't be a surprise. The passion that had raged between them in the past had always been hot, demanding, insatiable. And apparently, nothing had changed. Their bodies seemed to know right where they'd left off.

His hands sought the familiar contours of her back, but it wasn't enough, and he pulled her flush against a growing arousal.

A moan sounded low in Kristin's throat, and Joe was lost. Lost in a rushing swirl of desire he'd never really shared with anyone but Kristin. Not quite like this.

The kiss intensified, and when it seemed as though every lick of sense he'd ever mastered had suddenly taken a back seat to passion, Kristin pulled away.

Her cheeks were flushed. And a rosy splotch along the side of her neck and chest suggested she'd been as swept away as he had. She combed a hand through her hair and ran her tongue along swollen lips. "I'm really sorry, Joe. But I had no business kissing you like that. I don't know what got into me."

Joe knew what had gotten into her. But he wasn't going to spell it out. He'd never wanted a woman like he'd wanted Kristin Reynolds. And, at least in the past, it had seemed that she felt the same way.

"You don't need to apologize. It was my fault. I guess it was just the old memories playing havoc with my good sense." He dragged his hand through his hair, hoping the effort might clear his mind, dislodge the desire. But it didn't help. In fact, it merely made him feel guiltier about the forbidden kiss. "I'm not the kind of guy who would kiss another man's woman."

Before either of them could speak, a knock sounded. A sense of apprehension shoved against him, cornering him with no way out.

But there was nothing else he could do, other than face the interruption.

And pray it wasn't Allison.

But much to his dismay, when he swung open the front door, the attractive flight attendant stood on the porch, a bright-eyed smile on her face.

A smile that wouldn't last long.

"Surprised?" she asked.

Chapter Eight

Kristin studied the tall, attractive blonde who stood on Joe's porch holding the handle of a travel bag on wheels. She was apparently ready for a sleepover.

The afternoon sun glistened off strands of platinum in her shoulder-length hair. She smiled brightly, blue eyes dancing, as she released the handle of her suitcase and wrapped her arms around Joe's neck.

When the pretty blonde tried to place a kiss on his lips, he turned his head and offered her a cheek instead—a move that probably hurt the woman's feelings. It would have hurt Kristin's.

A big knot formed in Kristin's tummy, and her heart began to pound at an awkward pace, urging her to flee, while at the same time provoking her curiosity. For the life of her, she wasn't quite sure what was happening.

She and Joe had just shared a kiss—an inappropriate kiss for two people who were involved with other people. And *seriously* involved—at least in her case.

Yet she still felt awkward.

And hurt?

Yes.

No.

Make that confused and uneasy.

"What's the matter, Joe?" The blonde appeared bewildered by the way he'd sidestepped her kiss—until her gaze landed on Kristin. Shock, as well as annoyance, flared in her expression, and she crossed her arms. "I guess I should have called first."

"I can explain, Allison." Joe glanced at Kristin, and offered her an awkward grin that suggested he would try and explain things to her, too.

But how in the world could either of them explain the kiss they'd just shared?

Allison appeared to recover from her surprise, even if Kristin hadn't. "I'm a big girl, Joe. And I can add. Three's a crowd. So, if you don't mind, I'll just pick up my watch."

So it wasn't Chloe's watch that waited in Joe's kitchen. And since it was obvious the woman—Allison—wasn't Joe's housekeeper, Kristin did the math, too. And she was the one who didn't belong here.

"Allison," Joe said, "I want to introduce you to Kristin Reynolds, the mother of my son."

"Your son?" The blonde froze, her gaze flitting from the handsome fireman to Kristin and back again. "I didn't know you had a son."

"Neither did I. Come on in." Joe turned to Kristin. "This is Allison Winstead. The lady I've been dating."

Kristin's cheeks grew hot, and her tummy tossed and turned.

Didn't Joe feel the least bit guilty? Not about Kristin's presence, which he'd easily explained away, but about that kiss?

He appeared cool, calm and collected. Maybe he was used to juggling women and covering up his indiscretions.

On the other hand, Kristin didn't play those dating games. She picked up her purse from where she'd left it on the sofa. "Maybe I'd better come back another time. It was nice meeting you, Allison."

"Wait a minute," Joe said. "We haven't finished talking."

Kristin managed a smile. "Why don't we take care of our chat over the telephone? I don't want to put a damper on your evening plans."

Joe ran a hand through his hair, the first sign that he might be uncomfortable, then appealed to the blonde. "Kristin and I have to hash out some important details, and I don't want to do it over the phone. Can you please give us some time? You and I can get together later this evening."

Allison nodded. "Sure." Then she cast Kristin a smile that looked a bit forced.

"It was nice meeting you," Kristin repeated, although it wasn't.

"Same here. I'm sure we'll see each other again."

Kristin smiled and nodded, even though she wasn't looking forward to it. Not in the least.

Why must their lives be so complicated? Joe was already involved with a woman.

And she was involved with Dylan.

Involved?

She was engaged to marry him, for goodness sake. And she'd cheated on him.

It was only a kiss, of course. But it was of the hot, demanding, hungry variety. A prelude to sex.

Another layer of guilt settled heavily around Kristin's shoulders, nearly buckling her knees. How could she have done that to Dylan?

And it wasn't just the kiss she and Joe had shared that made her feel so guilty. It was also the memories and latent desire it had unleashed.

Not to mention the fact that she'd never felt that deep, blood-stirring arousal with anyone other than Joe Davenport.

And it wasn't fair.

Dylan loved her. And she loved him, too.

So why didn't his kisses turn her inside out? And why were her emotions tumbling out of control and out of reach?

Joe retrieved the bangle watch from the kitchen,

handed it to the pretty blonde. He brushed her cheek with his lips. "I'll talk to you later, Ally."

After the woman let herself out and closed the door, Joe turned to Kristin. "I'm sorry about that."

She was sorry, too. About a lot of things—some of which she couldn't even identify.

What had she and Joe just done? Cheated on their significant others? It didn't rest easy with her.

Was it bothering him, too?

"I'd rather not complicate things with Bobby by dating while he's visiting," Joe said. "And I have no intention of introducing him to Allison. At least, not yet."

Kristin nodded, taking comfort in that for some reason.

"Since you'll be taking Bobby back east at the end of summer, I'd like to spend as much time with him as I can over the next couple of months."

She nodded again. Where the heck were her words? They'd seemed to desert her, once she'd allowed that forbidden, soul-shattering kiss.

And the sooner she could forget it had ever happened, the better off she'd be.

Dylan had been pressuring her to set a date for their wedding, and for some reason, she'd been holding back. She'd used her father's health as an excuse, although now that she thought about it, her dad would probably feel much better just knowing her future was set and secure.

So maybe she ought to quit dragging her feet and do the right thing.

"By the way," she told the man who could still make her heart spin out of control. "Dylan and I will be setting a wedding date soon. And he'd like to spend our honeymoon in Europe. Maybe Bobby can stay with you."

"I'd…like that," Joe said, his voice soft, his words hesitant.

Had he been touched by her suggestion that he look after Bobby? Or bothered by her upcoming wedding?

Don't be foolish. Joe had stopped loving her years ago—if he'd ever loved her at all. And the kiss they'd just shared had been no big deal to him. Hadn't he brushed it aside as though it had never happened?

She needed to put it aside, too. And she needed to focus on Dylan. On their marriage. It would be best for everyone involved.

"Can I have Bobby on Friday?" Joe asked.

"Y-yes," she said, her voice coming out in a hesitant whisper. She cleared her throat and added, "That'll be fine. But I'd better get back home."

"I'll walk you outside."

"Don't bother." Kristin managed a smile, then let herself out, just as Allison had done.

While she climbed into the Town Car to drive away, a tear slipped down her cheek. She brushed it aside with a finger, only to have another take its place.

As she turned left, out of Joe's complex and onto the highway, her eyes were still teary. And to make matters worse, a big droplet of water splattered on the windshield. Then another.

Was it supposed to rain today? She hadn't heard the weather report.

Another splat landed, followed by two more.

As she pulled into the drive that led to the house, the sprinkles grew strong enough to require the windshield wipers. She flipped them on for a minute, getting a clear glimpse of several cars parked near the house. A silver Cadillac Seville. A white Lexus. A Lincoln Navigator. A sporty, red Mercedes.

Who was here? Her heart began to pound, as though it hadn't experienced an emotional workout just minutes ago.

What was going on?

She hit the button on the garage opener, then waited for the door to lift and parked the Town Car inside.

When she entered the house through the kitchen, she called, "Dad?"

"In here, honey."

She followed his voice to the den, where he was seated around a table, playing cards with several friends. Stacks of poker chips sat in front of each man.

"Kristin," her dad said with a grin. "You remember Dr. Dannenberg, don't you?"

"Yes, I do." She smiled at the silvery-haired gentleman to her father's left. "How are you, Doctor?"

Her dad's old college buddy, a retired surgeon, greeted her with a smile. "I'm going to stay the weekend and make sure your father takes his medicine. And a poker marathon is part of a new therapy I've developed."

Burl Wisnieski, the owner of several car dealerships in the county, laughed, as did Sam Bradley, a retired banker, and Darryl Niven, her father's investment counselor.

"I allowed Mrs. Davies to take Bobby to play with her niece's children for the evening," her father said. "And since I'm in good hands, why don't you drive up to L.A. and see Dylan?"

"But I came to Bayside to spend time with you," Kristin argued.

"Your dad has been worried about you since you've put your life on hold for him," Dr. Dannenberg said. "And so he invited me to stay a couple of days so you can take some time to yourself."

"That's right, honey." Her father grinned, his eyes crinkling with mirth. "Worrying about you can't possibly do me any good. Why don't you give me a break by going to L.A. and surprising Dylan?"

Kristin had to admit her father's mood had definitely improved, as had his coloring. Spending time with his friends certainly seemed to be therapeutic. In fact, seeing him like this, happy and playful, was comforting.

Maybe going to see Dylan wasn't a bad idea. It would certainly help get her mind back on track, where it belonged. On the future, rather than the past.

And the two-hour drive might help her come to grips with the changes Joe's involvement in Bobby's life was sure to bring.

Besides, it was time to set a wedding date and look to a future with the man who loved her.

Dylan would be pleased by her surprise visit. And she could certainly use some stability now. Not to mention, the reminder of his love.

She closed her eyes, trying to imagine herself wrapped in Dylan's arms. Surely that would help.

And maybe, if she threw her heart and soul into the relationship, her fiancé's kisses would send her senses reeling.

The way Joe's did.

Kristin arrived at the Las Palmas Resort, the five-star hotel in which Dylan was staying. She let the valet park her car, but resisted the bellman's request to carry her small overnight bag.

Once inside the lobby that was decorated in an elegant South Seas motif, she searched for a house phone.

She'd called Dylan on the way and, as she'd suspected, he was thrilled to learn she was driving up to visit and spend the night.

Too bad she didn't share his enthusiasm.

Her feelings for Dylan hadn't changed, of course. The kiss she'd shared with Joe was just playing havoc with her attitude. That's all.

Should she tell Dylan what she'd done? Tell him she'd let Joe kiss her, that she'd kissed him back—but just for old time's sake? That it didn't mean anything?

Maybe a confession and an apology would lead to forgiveness and set her world back on its axis. Dylan, of all people, would understand and be rational. Why, he'd probably explain the silly incident away, even if Kristin wasn't entirely sure why she'd allowed it to happen.

She picked up the house phone on a teakwood table by the lounge and asked to be put through to Dr. Montgomery's room. Dylan answered on the second ring.

"I'm in the lobby," she told him.

"Great. Do you want to come up? Or should I meet you for a cocktail before dinner?"

She glanced at the bar, which had begun to fill with hotel guests seeking evening relaxation. Maybe she ought to have Dylan come down here. After a drink, she could tell him what happened. Then he could rationalize what she'd done and forgive her. And then they'd be free to set the date of their wedding.

"Why don't you meet me in the lounge. I'd like to have a glass of wine to help me unwind from the drive."

"I'll be down shortly."

Normally, Kristin would have stood at the entrance to the lounge and waited. But her nerves had kicked up a notch. And she was eager to be seated in a corner booth.

"Dr. Montgomery will be meeting me," she told the dark-haired hostess who wore a colorful sarong.

"I know who he is," the woman said. "And as soon as the doctor arrives, I'll show him where you're sitting."

"Thank you."

Moments later, a waiter took Kristin's order. When Dylan was escorted to her table, she apologized for ordering without him.

"That's all right." He bent and brushed a kiss on her lips. A soft kiss. Warm and gentle.

Lukewarm and bland, a small voice whispered.

But Kristin refused to listen. Dylan wasn't the kind of man a woman compared to another. He was strong. Special. A man of his own making.

"How was the drive?" he asked.

"Not bad."

The waiter, who wore a Hawaiian shirt, brought a sterling silver bowl full of mixed nuts to the table and placed a chardonnay in front of her. Had she even requested a particular vineyard? She couldn't remember. She'd been too eager to hold on to the glass, to finger the cool, crystal spindle. To wash the butterflies out of her stomach.

"Can I get something for you to drink, Doctor?" the waiter asked.

"A vodka martini. Dry. Extra olives."

The young man nodded, then left the couple alone.

A ceiling fan circled overhead, much like the ones in any oceanfront restaurant on a tropical island, circulating the cool air in the room. Yet Kristin grew warm. Flushed. Uneasy.

A glance at Dylan told her he'd sensed her discomfort. "What's wrong?"

Explanations and excuses battered her mind. So did the urge to deny what he'd apparently seen in her expression, her demeanor.

She wanted to ignore the problem by saying: I love

you. I missed you. I wanted to spend the night with you. I've decided we need to set a date for our wedding.

Any of those comments would have pleased her fiancé. But she'd had her fill of lying and deception and hoped the old adage was true—that confession was good for the soul.

"Something happened today, Dylan. And although I'd like to sweep it under the table, I think it's best if I level with you."

Dylan took her hand in his, smiling and offering his love and support.

He was a good man. And he didn't deserve what she'd done to him. To them.

Oh, for Pete's sake, a small voice shrieked. *It was only a kiss. You certainly didn't make love with Joe.*

No. But while they'd kissed, while their tongues danced and their hands caressed, the memory of their lovemaking combined with a powerful flutter of swirling pheromones. And a renewed desire for her old lover—at least at that very moment—had been impossible to deny.

She glanced at the napkin under her glass and picked at the edge.

"Kristin?" Dylan gently squeezed the hand he held.

She looked up, caught his eye and decided to bare her soul. "I kissed Joe this afternoon."

"You what?" The sharp, unfamiliar tone of his voice reflected his surprise, his concern. And maybe a trace of anger.

She tucked a strand of hair behind her ear. "I'm not sure how it happened. But I kissed him. And I'm sorry."

"Why are you sorry?"

His question surprised her. And she hadn't been prepared to answer it. Her lips parted, and she sighed. "I'm sorry that it happened. I wouldn't want you kissing your old girlfriend. And I owe you an apology."

"I see."

Did he? She wasn't sure. *She* sure as heck didn't understand any of it. The kiss. The heat. The arousal it had provoked. The desire to kiss Joe again. The guilt.

"Let's talk about how that makes you feel," Dylan said, as though she were a patient in his office or one of the housewives who'd been chosen to be his guest on stage.

"No, Dylan," she said, wanting him to shed the robotic control and reveal the man inside. "Let's talk about how that makes *you* feel."

"Fair enough."

The waiter placed the martini in front of Dylan and asked, "Can I get you anything else?"

"That'll be all," Dylan told him. "Thank you."

When they were left alone, Kristin waited for him to speak. She watched as he lifted the glass, studied the colorless liquid, then set it down again. She waited as he withdrew the black plastic lance that held three big green olives, then popped it in his mouth and ate the olive at the tip.

For someone who wanted others to share their feelings, he was pretty tight-lipped. Was he angry? Hurt?

"Say something, Dylan."

"As a psychologist, I'm trying to understand. As a man, I'm hurt. Maybe even angry. And I'm worried. About us. Our future." He looked at her, revealing a human, flawed side of himself—a side he rarely displayed. "So we'll need to go back to the original question I asked you, only tweaking it a bit. How did the kiss affect you?"

"It made me feel cheap. And guilty."

"Why? Did it stir up old feelings for Joe? Old desires?"

She didn't answer, not sure she wanted to admit what that kiss had done to her—not even to herself.

"Come on, Kristin. He *is* the father of your son." Dylan stirred the stick of olives in his glass, then took a drink. "I'm not sure if I like the thought of competing with Joe Davenport for your affection."

Her conscience poked a rigid finger into her chest.

See? Some things, like those old feelings for Joe, should be locked away. The confession had merely opened an emotional Pandora's box.

She looked at Dylan, not at all liking the expression he wore, the look of being cornered. Crushed. Annoyed. Hurt.

"You don't have to compete with Joe. I'm not sure how or why the kiss happened. And like I said, I wouldn't have wanted you to kiss your old lover."

"And?" he asked, as though he was prodding a stubborn patient.

"I love you," she said, not entirely sure that she still did. Not entirely sure that she ever had. But she couldn't stand to see the disappointment she'd caused him. Nor could she imagine the reaction her father would have, should her perfect relationship with Dylan crumble.

A slow smile surfaced, crinkling his eyes and softening his expression. "Then, if it was a one-shot deal and it isn't going to happen again, I suppose it doesn't bother me."

She blew out the breath she'd been holding.

Wasn't she supposed to feel relieved now? Pardoned? Forgiven?

Yet, she still felt guilty. Unsure of herself. Unsure of him. Of them.

He'd dismissed it all very easily.

Of course, his calm, easygoing manner is what drew her to him in the first place. Not to mention his ability to understand emotions while being rational, calm and stable—reactions that didn't come easily for her father.

Yet now that same easygoing manner niggled at her, as did his lack of a passionate response.

Wasn't he the least bit jealous?

Oh, for crying out loud, Kristin. Thank your lucky stars that you have a man like Dylan in your corner, in your life.

Dylan relaxed in his seat, and took a slow, steady sip of his martini. "How's Bobby doing? I would imagine having Joe in his life is a bit new."

She nodded. "He seems to be happy. He still doesn't know who Joe is, though."

"And how do you feel about all of that?"

"I'm not used to sharing my son." She nibbled on her lip, holding back the part about believing Joe deserved to be a part of Bobby's life, in spite of how difficult it might be for her to be so involved with her old lover.

"This relationship they've embarked upon is still in a honeymoon period," Dylan said. "Just give it some time. Wait until Joe has to correct him or make him brush his teeth, clean his room and do his chores. Bobby could balk at future visits. And then we would have reason to curtail the time they spend together."

"You're probably right." She took another sip of wine.

They sat for nearly an hour, nursing their drinks. Talking about his day, the taping of the television show. Her father and his houseguest. The poker game that brought a smile and some color to her dad's face.

Never once did they bring up the kiss again, which should have made Kristin happy. But for some reason it didn't. Maybe because the memory still hovered around her, taunting her senses and reminding her that Dylan's kisses couldn't match Joe's.

And she hated herself each time that thought crossed her mind.

She glanced at the half-full glass of wine she'd been so eager to order, the wine that was supposed to make her feel better and had only made the knot in her stomach burn.

After Dylan paid the bill, he led her to the elevators so they could freshen up before dinner. They rode to the fifteenth floor and walked down the hall to his suite.

She waited as he opened the door, her heart beating louder and louder. The guilt prodded her to apologize again for good measure. Either that or make a mad dash out of the hotel and not look back.

Dylan let her inside the spacious room, then turned on the light. "It's so good to have you here."

She conjured a smile.

"I've missed you." He took her in his arms and kissed her. Warmly. Softly.

He urged her mouth open, and she accepted his tongue, hoping to fan the heat of his kiss.

But it was still warm. Still soft.

And as bland as an overcooked poached egg.

She pulled back.

"Honey?" His brow furrowed, and he frowned. "What's the matter?"

"I don't know. I can't do this. Not now. Not tonight. Maybe not ever. I'm not ready to get married."

"Why not?" he asked, his voice raised, apprehensive. "Because you kissed your old lover?"

"No." It was more than that. It was…because…she needed time alone. Time away from the men in her life—Dylan, her father. Joe. "I'm sorry, but I need to go."

"Don't be silly, honey. You've driven two hours to get here. It's raining." He took her by the hand. "Let's have dinner. Spend the night. We can talk about it in the morning."

She looked at the king-size bed and shook her head. "No. That's not a good idea. I need some time to think."

"You can think here—with me. I'll give you some space and time."

She shook her head and clutched the shoulder strap of her overnight bag. "No. I need to think alone."

As she turned the doorknob, he asked, "Where are you going?"

She had no idea. But she couldn't stay here.

Two hours later, Kristin continued to drive south, still not entirely sure where she was headed. Certainly not home to her father's house. He'd be more than disappointed that she'd returned. Alone.

The realization that her dad had actually orchestrated the visit with Dylan couldn't be dismissed. And she wasn't sure whether she should be annoyed or touched.

She continued her aimless drive, trying to sort through her feelings. If she'd grown tired, she would have pulled over and stopped at a hotel. As it was, she was too busy struggling with the jumbled emotions to feel weary.

And each time she glanced at her left hand, the weight and sparkle of the diamond engagement ring merely made her feel worse.

So why was she wearing it? She'd told Dylan she wasn't ready to marry him. Hadn't she? She slipped the ring off her finger and stashed it in her purse, just as her cell phone rang.

"Hello?"

"Kristin?"

It was Joe. What did he want? Before she could respond, the line crackled.

"Are you there?" he asked.

"Yes." She clutched the phone tight, holding it close to her ear, as though that could improve the reception.

"I'm sorry to bother you. I called your house, and your father said you'd gone to spend the night with Dylan. Can you talk? Or should I call back later?"

"Yes. I can talk."

"I want to apologize for Allison showing up like that. Bobby will always be a priority in my life. And so will you, for that reason."

Only for that reason?

Kristin shook off the senseless, adolescent emotions that had dogged her after that stupid kiss.

"I guess my call could have waited until you got home," he said. "But I was eager to make sure we had an understanding between us. Things were kind of… awkward today."

"That's okay. I understand."

"I don't just mean about Allison." He paused, as though choosing his words. "Are you with Dylan?"

"No. I'm not."

"Where are you? Whoa. Sorry about that. I guess that's none of my business."

"I'm driving around," she said. *And I have no idea when I'll stop.*

"By yourself?"

"Yes. I need some time to think."

"It's because of that kiss, isn't it?"

She didn't answer.

"Are you feeling guilty?"

Joe had always been able to read her, so it seemed fruitless to deny it. Besides, she was sick and tired of the lies, of covering up feelings that were perfectly normal. And acceptable. "Yes. I don't do things like that to people I care about."

The truth of her words and the lies she'd told her father came to mind, and she rolled her eyes.

"I'm sorry," Joe said. "I didn't mean for that kiss to affect you or your fiancé."

"Dylan was okay with it." She swallowed hard, not wanting to discuss it any further. "I just need some time alone. That's all."

But it wasn't all. Joe had hit upon her problem. And the kiss had affected her more than she wanted to admit.

"I don't know why it happened," he said. "It was just one of those things, instigated by a little nostalgia and curiosity, I suppose."

"You're right, of course. Why don't you give me a call tomorrow? Or later tonight."

"Where are you going to be?"

She hadn't decided yet. Not consciously, but as she glanced ahead and spotted a sign advertising the Bayside Inn and Marina, she flipped her turn signal. "I'm going to stay at the Bayside Inn, off Shoreline Drive."

Joe agreed to give her a call in an hour, then hung up, leaving her alone.

Just as she'd wanted.

Only she didn't feel any better about the kiss. Or the fact that she'd never gotten over Joe Davenport.

A man who didn't love her—even if his kiss suggested he could.

Chapter Nine

Joe glanced at the telephone receiver he still held in his hand. Kristin was going to stay at a hotel in Bayside tonight.

Alone.

No Dr. Dylan. No Thomas Reynolds. No one to disrupt a conversation about their son and his future, about important things like custody and visitation. Things parents needed to work out on their own.

Did he dare show up at the hotel and insist they come to some kind of working agreement about Bobby?

He was on duty for the next couple of days, which would prolong the time they could settle things between them.

And while they were at it, they probably ought to talk about the kiss, because it was undoubtedly bothering her. Heck, to be honest, it had affected him, too.

He'd had other lovers, and sex had always been good. But no woman had ever been able to stir his blood like Kristin had once done.

Like she was still able to do.

He cursed under his breath. Not even Ally, as pretty and personable as she was, as warm and willing, could make his blood rage or make his heart swell in his chest.

After Kristin had left this afternoon, he'd gone over to talk to Allison, to tell her he wanted to put a hold on their budding romance for a while—just until Bobby went back to the east coast with his mother.

She hadn't taken it very well and said she might not be able to wait for him to make a commitment to her, which hadn't bothered him as badly as she'd probably expected it to. But that was okay with him.

What really bothered him was that things had become strained and more awkward between him and the mother of his son. And *that* was something he wanted to correct—no matter how moving Kristin's kiss had been. No matter how damn arousing.

He glanced at his watch. Just past eight o'clock.

If he went to see her at the Bayside Inn, what was the worse thing that could happen?

She could tell him to leave.

And if she didn't? They could have that much needed talk.

He gave the idea about ten minutes to stew, then grabbed his car keys and headed out into a dark, wet night.

The rain pounded on the windshield of his Tahoe, as he drove down the interstate, looking for the Shoreline Drive exit. It wasn't a good night to be on the road, but neither was it an evening he wanted to spend alone—not when he and Kristin had so much to talk about, so much to decide.

He blew out a sigh. That kiss had been a humdinger, especially since they'd both been fully dressed and standing.

Kristin had said Dylan was okay with it. Of course, Joe couldn't understand why she'd tell the guy something like that. It seemed like a counterproductive thing to confess in a relationship—especially one that was marriage-bound.

If the tables were turned and Joe had been her fiancé, he'd have flipped out if Kristin had kissed an old lover.

But she'd said the "relationship expert" was *okay* with it, so who was Joe to argue.

And speaking of good ol' Dr. Dylan, why wasn't Kristin cuddling with him in bed on a night made for loving? Did that mean *she* wasn't okay with the kiss?

A smile tugged at his lips. He knew what it had done to her physically; he could still hear the soft sounds of her whimper. But had it messed with her mind? Made her feel as if she'd done something wrong?

Maybe he was reading too much into it. After all, Dylan didn't care. But Joe still found that hard to believe.

Of course, Kristin might have lied about her fiancé's reaction.

Nah. She was too honest. And Dr. Dylan was too polished, too sure of himself and his diplomas to be insecure in his relationship with Kristin. Besides, it didn't take a psychologist to know what kind of man Thomas Reynolds wanted for a son-in-law. And it sure as hell wasn't the son of a convicted drug dealer.

In spite of Joe's intent to leave those old memories buried, he couldn't stop their resurrection. Couldn't help remembering when Kristin had been his.

He'd been naive back then—when he was on the cusp of adulthood. And he'd been so much in love with Kristin that he'd actually nursed a belief of forever and happy-ever-after. How crazy was that?

Reynolds would have blown his top sky-high if he'd found out Joe Davenport had been his daughter's first lover.

Hell, the old man probably still would.

And that was another thing he and Kristin needed to discuss. Her father and that blasted secret that made Joe want to slam his fist into a wall.

He wasn't sure how long it could remain a secret. Dr. Dylan and Allison knew. And following the barbecue, Harry had mentioned the resemblance he'd seen between Joe and Kristin's son.

What did Kristin expect Joe to do? Lie to the man who'd been a father to him? No way. Especially when Harry knew how much Joe had loved Kristin, how involved they'd been. And what a hard-ass her old man had been—five years *after* the fire.

Joe turned right, through the palm-lined drive that led to the main entrance of the Bayside Inn. He wasn't sure how Kristin would react when he showed up at the hotel. Probably run him off, since she'd made no secret of wanting to be alone.

A wave of apprehension struck. Would she be angry at his surprise visit?

Oh, what the hell. She'd never been one to stay mad at him for long. Not like her grudge-holding old man.

Once inside the lobby, Joe called Kristin's room and told her where he was. "Can you come down and talk to me? Or should I come to your room? It doesn't matter, as long as I can have a few minutes of your time."

She paused before asking, "Why?"

"I'd like to make sure things are settled between us and I have a feeling you're bothered by me…and the past." He cleared his throat. "I want to make you feel better."

He rolled his eyes at the way his words had come out. Would she understand what he meant? Cripes, he was at her hotel, asking to come to her room and make her feel better. But that's not what he meant. She was obviously stressed about something. And the kiss seemed like a logical culprit. Joe, better than anyone, ought to be able to help.

Better than Dr. Dylan had been able to do? Maybe not, but he would come up with another game plan if need be.

He ran a hand through the rain-dampened strands of his hair. His shirt and jeans had gotten wet, too. Maybe he shouldn't have come here.

"I'm in Room 312," she said.

The ball was in his court now. He just hoped he could keep it in bounds.

Moments later, he stood before her room and knocked. She opened the door, but didn't step aside, and he didn't force the issue. He was too caught up by her appearance, her presence.

She stood in the muted, hotel-room light, with her hair bound in a white, towel-wrapped turban and wearing one of those fluffy courtesy robes. She'd showered and looked damn near ready for bed.

The tropical scent of her lotion and soap taunted him in a way he hadn't anticipated, and the sexual memories of their past hovered over him.

Her fingers twiddled with the lapel of her robe, revealing the skin of her throat and chest.

No nightgown?

Ah, cut it out, Davenport. You'll never get things said and settled if you don't keep your libido in check.

"Can I come in and sit down?" he asked.

She stepped aside and motioned to a desk chair. He took it, and she sat on the edge of the bed.

When she crossed her legs, a knee slipped through the robe, revealing a glimpse of thigh. She tugged at the robe to cover herself. But it was too late. He'd already seen enough to start his blood pumping and his mind reeling like a thirteen-year-old kid caught in the throes of his first adolescent crush.

"I'm sorry about the kiss," he said without thinking. Ah, hell. He hadn't meant to start with that, but it was obvious that it stood between them like an insurmountable wall.

"You told me that already," she said. "And I apologized, too."

"I know. But I don't like the trouble it's caused you."

She parted her lips, as if to argue…or maybe to agree, but she didn't respond, letting him draw his own conclusions.

"I guess that's why it's tough for old lovers to be friends," he added, trying to shrug it off. But it wasn't working.

Renewed desire merged with memories of all they'd shared, creating a sexual intensity that was almost palpable.

She continued to watch him, waiting. Looking far more attractive than he'd ever seen her. More appealing. More arousing. Pure Kristin—unadorned.

"We had something special at one time," Joe said, breaching the wall he ought to steer clear of. "And it's only normal for our bodies to react to the memories."

Slow down, he told himself. Tiptoe or you might pull the pin on an emotional hand grenade that could blow up in your face.

But he couldn't seem to stop.

Seeing Kristin in next to nothing and perched on a

king-size bed only made him want to close the distance between them, to run his knuckles along her cheek. To reach inside her robe and claim what had once been his. Was she feeling it, too?

She was all eyes—like a deer in a meadow, cautious and ready to bolt. It tore at him to see her like that. On edge. Alert, but vulnerable.

He wished he had Dylan's training so that he could say the right thing to her. Something that would put them both on an even keel. But then again, the TV shrink must have crashed and burned. If he hadn't, he'd be with her now, seeing her fresh from the shower. Covered by a robe that was tied at the waist. One little tug on that sash…

Get a grip, Davenport. Cut to the chase.

"I'm attracted to you, Kristin. I always have been. And I figure you feel that way, too. But that doesn't mean either of us have to take advantage of the attraction. If we both put Bobby's welfare above all else— our feelings, our disappointments—then we should be able to put the past aside. Even the immediate past." He offered her an olive-branch smile. "What do you say?"

Kristin studied the man who'd once been her lover. His wet, tousled hair needed a comb. But she found it incredibly arousing to have him sitting in her room, his clothing still bearing signs of the rain that continued to dance upon the windows.

In a way, it was touching that he'd come to see her

in spite of the weather. That he cared enough to address the issues that faced them. "You're right, Joe. All that matters is Bobby."

He leaned forward in the desk chair and rested his elbows on damp, denim-clad knees. He still had that rebellious way about him that she found so attractive, so stimulating. And the fact that she sat before him with only a robe to hide her body didn't help.

"How's your dad doing?" he asked.

"He seemed pretty chipper tonight." She touched the towel on her head. Realizing it had listed to one side, she tried to right it.

"When do you think we can tell him?"

So, Joe's concern about her father's health was self-serving. But she supposed she couldn't blame him for that. "I told you before. I don't want my dad to know until his health is more stable."

Joe tensed, then sat up straight. "Then how about letting me tell Bobby?"

"No. He's too close to my dad. He'd say something."

"And then all hell would break loose." Joe sat back and crossed his arms. "Is that it?"

She nodded. That's exactly what would happen, and she wasn't ready for it.

"Kristin, why do I get the feeling that you wouldn't tell your dad about me, even if his health was perfect?"

She wanted to argue, to deny it. But in a sense, there was a certain amount of truth to what Joe had said. She'd always been the apple of her father's eye, his only child. And she'd lied to him. Over and over again. She wasn't ready to disappoint him with the truth of her deceit. "Like I said, I'll tell him after his surgery."

"I'm not happy about that decision, but I'll abide by it—for now, anyway. But I want to be involved in Bobby's life. Not just the outings we've been having. I want to be included in the decisions about what's best for him, like what school he's going to attend and whether he can play Pop Warner Football. I want to be a father in every sense."

Kristin wasn't sure she wanted to consider Joe's wishes on every parental issue, but she would—as a compromise. And maybe because it was the right thing to do. "I'll agree to that."

"Thanks." Joe stood. "I won't keep you any longer. It looks as though you're ready for bed."

She followed him to the door in an effort to be polite. Or maybe, if she'd start being more honest with herself, it was in an attempt to prolong his visit, no matter how unsettling it was.

He stopped beside the glassed wardrobe mirror and turned. Their gazes met, and sexual awareness held them fast.

She gripped the sides of her robe, her nails digging into the plush, white cotton. She had to force herself not to touch him. Not to breathe. Not to tell him that one of the reasons the kiss had bothered her was because she wanted it to happen again.

He cupped her cheek, sending a spiral of heat to her core.

She was strong enough not to provoke a kiss. But was she strong enough to resist if he pushed for one?

She hoped so, but she couldn't trust her rebellious body. A body he'd once known intimately. A body that still ached for him.

His thumb brushed her cheek, and her knees nearly buckled.

"Kristin, I never want to disrupt your life or cause you problems. Not with your dad, and not with Dylan. I just want to be a father to my son."

"I…understand." And she did. It pleased her to know Joe cared about Bobby and wanted to be a part of his life. She just hoped she could allow him into her world without losing her heart in the bargain. Unless she'd done so already.

"Let's put that kiss behind us."

She nodded, hoping she could.

"Sleep tight." He ran his knuckles along her cheek, then turned and let himself out.

After the door closed, she fingered the spot where her face and skin still tingled.

"Good night," she whispered. But she didn't believe she'd sleep tight. Too much had happened.

And too much hadn't.

Kristin had slept like hell that night. At five in the morning, she'd checked out of the hotel and driven home. She'd even managed to let herself in quietly without waking her father, his friend or Bobby.

As far as anyone knew, she'd gone to L.A. and returned early.

Her luck held—until nine o'clock, when Dylan knocked at the door.

"Good morning." He brushed a kiss across her lips. "I postponed the meeting I had with the network execs, telling them it was a family emergency."

She struggled with the idea of telling him to go away and give her more time, which didn't seem fair. So she stepped aside and let him inside.

"Are you feeling better?" he asked.

She supposed so. The visit with Joe had helped in some ways. At least the guilt no longer plagued her. She'd loved Joe once and couldn't help it if her body still reacted to his touch. The only thing that made her feel guilty was her engagement to Dylan, something she'd tried to end last night, even if Dylan might not have taken her seriously. "Yes, I do feel better. Thanks."

"You don't look as though you slept very well."

She ignored his observation, since she was trying to put it all behind her, as Joe had suggested. "Would you like a cup of coffee?"

"Yes. Please." He followed her into the kitchen, then sat at the table while she served him. "Your father's health has put undue stress on you."

That was true. But there was more going on than that.

"And I imagine Joe's growing obsession with Bobby has been a worry, too."

She bristled. Dylan was usually so thoughtful, so observant. And his criticism of Joe seemed unwarranted, unfair. Especially when she understood Joe wanting to spend time with his son before the new school year started. "I think you're being far too clinical and harsh. I haven't found Joe's interest in Bobby to be obsessive."

Dylan blew out a ragged sigh. "Okay. Maybe I resent him more than I care to admit. But I love you, Kristin. And I have every intention of giving you time to work through things. And if you don't want to set a wedding date or even consider us engaged, that's all right with me. I'll wait until you're ready."

"What if I'm never ready?" she asked, not at all sure she would be. And sorry that might be the case. Her father really liked Dylan. And she liked him, too, even if she questioned her love for him.

"I'm going to wait out your confusion and support you through your father's surgery."

"I appreciate that. You're a good man." And he was. But that didn't mean she'd changed her mind about marrying him.

Dylan reached across the table and took her hand, his thumb brushing across the finger that had once worn his ring. His gaze caught hers, but he didn't ask what she'd done with it. Or why she'd taken it off.

She answered anyway. "I feel better not wearing it now."

"That's fine."

She withdrew her hand from his grasp, just as Bobby entered the kitchen with a sheet of paper in his hands.

"What have you got there?" Kristin asked her son.

Bobby handed her a sketch he'd drawn with a black crayon. No red, no blue, no yellow, no green.

"That's an interesting picture," Dylan said. "Why don't you tell me about it."

"This is Joe and me playing Nintendo." Bobby pointed out characters on the sofa. Neither was smiling.

"That's nice," Kristin told her son, although it was pretty ugly. "Do you want me to put it on the refrigerator?"

"If you want to. Can I have a cookie?"

"Of course." She reached into the plastic container for one of the Snickerdoodles she and Mrs. Davies hid from her father.

"Can I eat it outside?" Bobby asked.

"Sure." She handed him a sugar-and-cinnamon-crusted treat.

"Thanks, Mom." Then he dashed out the back door.

Dylan cleared his throat. "Kristin, I hate to add more stress at a time like this, but I'm concerned about the morbid color scheme in that picture Bobby drew."

A flood of apprehension swept over her, as it usually did whenever Dylan pointed out an error in her way of thinking. "Why?"

"Happy children draw birds and rainbows, bright yellow suns." Dylan nodded at the artwork she held. "That gothic sketch could be a manifestation of something serious, something deep-seated. A relationship with Joe may not be what's best for Bobby."

Kristin furrowed her brow, and her stomach, which seemed to be unusually sensitive lately, knotted.

Dylan had a doctorate in psychology and had gained the respect of readers and audiences all over the country. How could she not take his concerns seriously?

"I think you ought to curtail the time Bobby and Joe spend together until we can have him assessed by a child psychologist."

"I don't know," Kristin said. "Bobby seems so happy when he comes home from being with Joe."

"Maybe he's sensed that your father is seriously ill. And that you've been worried. Adding a relationship with Joe, at this time, might not be in his best interest."

"I'll keep an eye on him," she said. "He and Joe have another outing scheduled this weekend."

Dylan furrowed his brow. "Can't you think of a way to postpone it?"

"No. Not this time." She suspected Dylan was surprised by her decision, since she'd readily taken his advice in the past. But this was the kind of thing she'd agreed to discuss with Joe.

"Then let me set up an appointment with one of my colleagues."

"I'd like to wait on that, if you don't mind."

"Don't wait too long, honey."

Surely Dylan was overreacting. Kristin had a great deal of respect for his understanding of human relationships, but a small maternal voice insisted Bobby wasn't manifesting anything.

Was that merely wishful thinking on her part?

Possibly. But something didn't sit right.

Could Dylan be biased? Was it possible that he was trying to curtail Bobby's contact with Joe so that he could limit Kristin's involvement with her old lover as well?

No, of course not. Dylan wasn't the least bit insecure and was far above that kind of thing. He was merely trying to help.

Still, this was the sort of thing Joe would want to know. But if she told him, she wasn't sure how he'd react.

And all she needed was more stress in her life.

That evening, when Kristin's father realized she wasn't going to invite Dylan to sleep in the guest room, he'd taken her aside and asked what had gotten into her.

"Nothing," she snapped. Then trying to regroup, she added, "I'm not comfortable with him sleeping here."

Her father's brow furrowed, his displeasure evident. "Why not?"

"Just because. Let it go, Daddy. Please?"

He'd grumbled under his breath, but he let Dylan return to L.A. without any further comment.

The remainder of the evening had been low-key, and at nine o'clock they'd all gone to bed.

Now, hours later, the house was quiet, but Kristin couldn't sleep. She'd tossed and turned like a beached flounder, unable to find a comfortable spot.

Exhausted, yet wide-awake, she threw off the covers and padded into the kitchen to make some chamomile tea. While the water heated, she retrieved a teacup and saucer from the china hutch in the dining room.

She studied the delicate pink-carnation pattern of the set that had once belonged to her maternal grandmother. Mama used to enjoy tea in the evening and had often invited Kristin to join her. Of course, Kristin's cup had been filled mostly with lightly sweetened cream, but the memory was one of the few she had of her mom.

On the east wall, a large painting of her mother graced the formal room. Eleanor Reynolds stood barefoot in the sand, a white sundress billowing softly in the breeze. She wore a wistful smile—a dreamy smile.

At least, that's what Kristin had always imagined.

Had it been a wry smile? A sign of unhappiness?

Sometimes Kristin could remember her mother sitting at the kitchen table, a cup of tea in hand, her face red and splotchy, her eyes watery.

"They're just happy tears, Krissy. I can't believe how lucky I am that God blessed me with a little girl like you."

Kristin had accepted the explanation as a child. But as an adult? She wasn't so sure.

When Mama was still alive, her father hadn't been around much. Had her parents been happy? Had her dad's kisses weakened her mother's knees? Or had they merely been nice and comforting?

Had they had a happy marriage? Had they laughed

and enjoyed walks along the bay? Or had her father been too busy?

She shrugged off the questions she'd never have answered and carried the teacup back to the kitchen, where Bobby's black drawing was displayed on the fridge.

Was it a sign that her child was troubled?

Dylan thought so. But it wasn't Dylan's opinion she wanted. It was Joe's. And in spite of the hour, she picked up the phone and called her son's father.

The phone rang, jarring Joe from a sound sleep. He fumbled for the receiver, then barked out, "Hello?"

"It's me. Kristin."

He sat up in bed and dragged a hand through his hair. Squinting, he checked the red numerals on the alarm clock—12:17. "What's the matter? Is Bobby all right?"

"Yes. I think so."

"What's on your mind, honey?" He blew out a sigh when he realized the endearment had slipped out.

"Bobby drew a picture today."

He scrunched his face and again looked at the clock. He'd told her he wanted to be involved in Bobby's life. But couldn't this wait until morning?

"He drew it in black, Joe. No other colors."

"So?"

"Don't you find that a bit odd? Kind of dark and morbid?"

Joe shrugged. "Not really. Do you?"

"Well, Dylan said it could be a sign that something was bothering him. And I'm concerned."

Joe never had put much stock in television shrinks, and the more he thought about Dylan's assumption, the more determined he was to get more involved in his son's life. "Can't you talk to Bobby's pediatrician?"

"Yes, I suppose so. But Dylan suggested we schedule a full psychological evaluation."

"Now, wait a minute. That guy may have written a couple of books and might be charming audiences around the country, but I've spent a lot of time with Bobby, and he seems normal. And happy. If something was bothering him, I think I'd know."

"I'm glad you feel that way. I thought Dylan had overreacted."

"You know, I'm not going to tell you who to marry, Kristin. But I'm not impressed with the guy." Joe hadn't meant to pressure her again—so soon—but he couldn't seem to help himself. "If Bobby is bothered by something, maybe it's your relationship with that damn shrink. Maybe Bobby likes the guy about as much as I do. And maybe he senses that I'm his father and he's mad about being lied to."

When she didn't respond, he added, "If we could tell him the truth…"

"I can't do that yet."

"You said we could tell him when the time was right. But as far as I'm concerned, the time is now."

"I didn't call to argue."

Joe raked a hand through his hair again. "I know. I'm sorry. It's just tough."

"I know."

"What did your dad have to say about it?" Joe asked, surprised that he cared what Thomas Reynolds thought.

"I haven't told him."

"Are you protecting your old man?" he asked. "Or still living under his thumb?"

"I'm protecting him. And I'm trying to protect Bobby. That's why I called."

Joe felt like a jerk. And a fool. She'd appealed to him as Bobby's father, something he'd wanted her to do. "I'm sorry, Kristin. I really appreciate you calling to get my opinion. I'm just being overly sensitive, I guess. If you want to have Bobby see a psychologist, that's fine. But I don't think there's anything bothering him."

"I was thinking the same thing."

"Can I pick him up on Friday, as planned?"

"Yes. He'll be ready."

Joe looked at the clock—12:24. "Why aren't you asleep?"

"No reason," she said. "No reason at all."

He didn't buy that. But, then again, whatever might be going on in her personal life wasn't his business.

Not even if a small part of him wished it were.

Chapter Ten

On Saturday afternoon, Kristin brought Bobby to Joe's place, since she had errands to run.

Or at least, that's what she'd said. Joe still had the feeling she wanted to keep him away from her house, if at all possible.

After Bobby went inside, she remained on the porch. The simple black dress she wore wasn't anything remarkable, yet her classy aura gave it a style of its own.

"Would you like to go along with us?" Joe asked. "We'll probably see a movie."

"Sounds like fun." Kristin tucked a glossy strand of hair behind her ear, revealing a good-size diamond stud, and smiled. "But I need to pick up some groceries and go to the drugstore for my dad."

She looked especially pretty for a woman going to the market. And he thought about saying something to that effect, but he figured she might not want to be reminded that he found her attractive.

"I hope you have a good time at the movies," she said. "What are you going to see?"

"Go Home, Mutt." He shrugged, still feeling a bit out of his element with the parenting stuff but trying his darnedest to do the right thing. "It's supposed to be good for families with children. One of my buddies at the fire station has three kids, and that's what he suggested."

"Good choice." She stood there, just a moment longer than necessary. At least it seemed that way.

A midday breeze caught her jasmine-laced perfume and mingled with the rush of pheromones that swirled in the air whenever she was near. The arousing scent tempted him to make a move. Instead, he hooked his thumbs in the front pockets of his faded jeans.

"Well," she said, dragging out the word. "I've got a lot to get done, so, I'd better go."

"I'll drop him off later, if that's okay."

"That'll be fine." She offered him a dimpled smile that sent a warm, squirmy jolt to his gut and a zap to his heart.

"Is five o'clock okay?"

She nodded, then turned and walked back to the white Town Car. Her hips swayed, and the hem of her black dress brushed the back of shapely calves, taunting him with what wasn't his any longer.

It took all he had to shut the door to block his view. But he rallied. He had no claim on her; he never really did. And if she suspected he was having trouble keeping his eyes off her, she might curtail his time with his son.

Besides, he was glad that she felt comfortable enough to leave Bobby with him, especially after Dr. Shrink's assessment of the boy's black-crayon drawing. But something still ate at him.

He couldn't shake the feeling that Kristin was avoiding him. And that she hadn't really put the kiss behind them.

Actually, he hadn't been able to shake it, either, although he'd be damned if he'd let her know.

"Hey, Bobby," Joe said, focusing on reality, on what he could claim as his. "The movie starts in twenty minutes."

"Okay! Let's go."

More than two hours later, as they strolled out of the Moonlight Cinema in downtown Bayside, Bobby chuckled. "That was a really cool movie."

Joe hadn't been excited to sit through the latest full-length cartoon, since he preferred action flicks. But he had to admit it was pretty entertaining while providing a moral lesson. "You're right. In fact, it was much better than I expected."

Even the adults in the audience did their share of laughing and rooting for the scruffy dog who'd been homeless until the end.

"I really liked the part where Barney swam into the lake to save the little girl," Bobby said. "And then he got to live with a real family."

"That was my favorite part, too." Joe placed a hand on his son's shoulder. He wasn't ready for their day to end and head home. "How about an ice cream cone?"

"I'm kind of full from all the popcorn and that big soda, but I can squeeze in some ice cream, if it's chocolate."

Joe smiled. "Attaboy."

They continued down the sidewalk, past Grandma Jane's Kitchen, a down-home café that was famous for its chicken-fried steak. And past We're Stylin', the only hair salon in Bayside.

The ice cream parlor sat on the main drag, next to Bayside Trust and Savings, a bank that catered to the city bigwigs. After giving Bobby a talk about looking both ways, even in a crosswalk, they made their way across the street.

A bell on the door chimed when they entered the shop that boasted a Gay Nineties decor in colors of red and white. Moments later, Joe ordered double-scoop chocolate cones.

When they'd been served, they slid onto the red-vinyl seat of a booth in back, then ate while talking about Bobby's hope for a puppy of his own—a wish, no doubt, triggered by the movie they'd just watched.

As a kid, Joe'd had a dog. Sort of. Good ol' Buster was a stray who hung out in the alley near the run-down apartment in which he'd lived. His old man wouldn't let him bring the dog inside, but that didn't mean that sweet, scrawny mutt and Joe weren't the best of friends. Or that Joe couldn't slip him food and water whenever his dad was passed out on the sofa or took off on one of those two- or three-day parties.

In fact, Joe wouldn't mind having a puppy now, one Bobby could claim whenever he came to visit. But he lived in a condominium. And with his schedule, it wouldn't be fair to the animal.

But that didn't mean he and Bobby couldn't find something else to share.

"Come on," Joe said. "Let's go check out the hobby shop. Maybe we can find a project that'll be fun for us to work on together."

"Sure." Bobby scooted from his seat, licking the side of the bottom scoop and snagging a dab of chocolate with his nose.

Joe laughed, then grabbed a couple of napkins from the dispenser on the table and dabbed at the small freckled nose that was shaped just like his own.

Bobby looked up at him like he was some kind of superhero.

It tickled Joe to be held in such esteem, but it was the bright-eyed smile that caught his eye. That wasn't the kind of grin a troubled kid wore. Not that Joe was any expert. But wouldn't he sense it if something sad and dark were brewing beneath Bobby's surface?

Dylan had made a big deal about that black-crayon drawing. But there was no way that Bobby was manifesting anything, other than what could be considered normal for a boy his age.

Of course, that didn't mean there wasn't something bugging him at home.

Deciding to probe a bit, Joe asked, "How do you like being in Bayside for the summer?"

"It's really cool. I get to play every day since I don't have to go to school. And I get to live with my grandpa, which is neat 'cause I don't get to see him very often."

"That's great." Joe ushered the boy outside, wondering how far to push. Well, he'd take it one step at a time. "I guess it's also cool that you're so close to L.A. That way, you can see Dr. Dylan more often."

"Yeah. I guess." Bobby kicked at the sidewalk. "But he's my mom's friend. Not mine."

Joe's ears perked up. Even though he wanted his son to be happy with his mother's choice of men, a selfish side of him wanted the boy to think the know-it-all doctor was a jerk. "You don't like Dylan?"

"He's okay—for a grown-up. But I like you better. You're more fun to be with. And you don't tell me what to do all the time." Bobby slipped a hand in Joe's.

As the small fingers gripped him tight, Joe's heart nearly leaped right out of his chest.

He cleared his throat, hoping to make room for the words to come out. "Thanks, Bobby. I've enjoyed being with you, too. In fact, I'd like for us to stay friends, even after your mom takes you back home to start school."

The towheaded kid shot him a glowing smile that

damn near knocked him off the pedestal on which he'd found himself temporarily placed. "Really? Will you come and visit me?"

"Sure. And maybe your mom will let you come spend time with me, too."

"That would be way cool! On the plane when we came out here, Mom and I saw a kid fly all by himself. And the airplane people were really nice to him, giving him extra dessert and making sure he could see the movie."

"Let's see what your mom thinks about that. If she'd worry, I'd fly out and get you."

"You'll probably have to come get me then." Bobby scrunched up his face. "My mom worries a lot. But how could a kid get lost on an airplane?"

Joe had a feeling Kristin wouldn't be too eager to send Bobby by himself on a cross-country flight. But it was something to look forward to. "When it gets closer to the time you'll have to go home, we'll talk to her about it."

They'd just begun the short walk to the hobby shop when two men walked toward Bayside Trust and Savings. Joe didn't recognize the guy in the blue suit. But Kristin's dad was difficult to miss.

"Hey!" Bobby pulled his hand from Joe's and waved. "There's my grandpa!"

Thomas Reynolds turned at the sound of the boy's voice. He smiled broadly, until he caught sight of Joe.

"Come on." Bobby took Joe's hand again and pulled

him toward the man who wore a gray three-piece suit and more than a fair share of resentment on his face. "I want to show you to my grandpa."

While Bobby introduced Joe to his grandfather, not realizing the two men had known and disliked each other for years, Reynolds managed a brittle smile—for the boy's sake, no doubt. So Joe conjured up an insincere one of his own.

The younger man standing to the side of Reynolds stretched out a hand in greeting. "How do you do? I'm Darryl Niven."

"Joe Davenport."

"Nice to meet you." If Mr. Niven realized Reynolds had an issue with Joe and wasn't up for cursory introductions, he didn't show it.

Reynolds seemed to struggle with putting on a happy front for Bobby's sake—an impossible task, it seemed, as his cool, gray eyes traveled from father to son, then back again.

Had he noticed the resemblance that seemed obvious to Joe? The same topaz-colored eyes that Harry Logan had spotted?

It was hard to say.

Reynolds placed a gentle hand on the top of his grandson's head, his fingers caressing the wheat-colored strands. "I'll see you back at the house, Bobby. Mr. Niven and I are on our way to a meeting."

"Okay. Bye, Grandpa."

As Mr. Niven headed toward the glass door, Reynolds peered over his shoulder, taking one last look at Joe. He pursed his lips, then entered the bank.

But the chill of his gaze followed Joe all the way to the hobby shop, with no sign of letting up.

That evening, Bobby jabbered a mile a minute about Joe, the movie and a model plane they were going to build that would really fly.

Kristin, her heart warmed by her son's enthusiasm, still found it difficult to believe a relationship with Joe had caused him any undue stress. Still, Dylan's concerns were impossible to ignore.

Did the black drawing signify something dark in Bobby's life?

Had he picked up on her own confusion? Her own worries and fears?

Kids did that sometimes. And she didn't need a degree in psychology to know that.

She glanced at her father, noting his silence, the solemn expression on his face.

What was bothering him?

Probably the fact that Bobby seemed to idolize Joe.

But holding his tongue was unusual, and she suspected he was just biding his time, waiting until Bobby went to bed to roar out a complaint.

Talk about stress. If given a black crayon, Kristin could easily sketch a dark, morbid mural on the family room wall.

But she was no fool. When it was time for Bobby to

go to bed, she was going to retire to her room, as well, making a confrontation impossible.

Those tirades weren't good for her father's blood pressure or his heart. And quite frankly, even if his health had improved dramatically, she'd grown tired of listening to him rave.

Especially about Joe Davenport.

"Come on, Bobby." Kristin stood and reached out a hand. "Let's you and I get ready for bed."

Her gaze skimmed over her father, where he was seated in his black-leather easy chair. And she caught his eye, his expression.

If she didn't know better, she'd think he suspected there was more to Joe's involvement with Bobby than met the eye.

But maybe that was merely her imagination.

And her guilt.

Just after lunch, Joe and Sam Henley inspected the equipment on Old Red, the hook and ladder that had been with the department for years.

When a white Lincoln Town Car drove up, Joe cracked a smile, assuming Kristin and Bobby had stopped by. But when he spotted Thomas Reynolds behind the wheel, he sobered.

Kristin's father climbed from the car, wearing a harsh, barren expression and a don't-mess-with-me stance. His eyes narrowed when they landed on Joe. "Can I have a minute of your time, Davenport?"

"Go ahead," Sam told Joe. "I'll finish here."

Joe nodded, then joined Reynolds by his car. "What's up?"

"Suppose you tell me."

Hadn't Kristin told her dad that Joe was seeing Bobby? That the fireman had taken an interest in the boy? "I'm not sure I know what you're talking about."

"Have you noticed how much my grandson looks like you?"

Joe shrugged. He sure wished Kristin were standing here. That she could take over and either perpetuate the lie or tell him the truth. At this point, it didn't seem to matter which. It wasn't Joe's place to tell her old man anything.

Reynolds stepped closer, gunmetal-gray eyes aimed at Joe. "Are you Bobby's father?"

"Isn't that a question you ought to ask Kristin?"

"I did. More than seven years ago." Reynolds tensed his lips and stroked his left arm.

"What did she tell you?"

"She said Bobby's father was a water polo player at the college she attended."

Joe fisted his hands at his sides, released them, then crossed his arms. He wanted to lash out and slam Reynolds with the truth. But he'd made a promise to Kristin. "Then that ought to answer your question."

"It did. Until I saw you and Bobby standing side by side."

Joe contemplated gently telling the man the truth,

confessing that he was Bobby's father. That he might not have had a decent dad of his own, but he wanted to be a part of his son's life. But he held tight to the promise he'd made Kristin.

The old man's face reddened, and his eyes glared. "Aren't you going to say something in your defense? Hell, I paid all my daughter's medical expenses back then. Bobby's, too. And I sent checks to supplement her income, to replace the child support that never came."

Joe wanted to punch a fist in the man's face. To defend himself. To say that Bobby's birth had been a surprise to him, too.

Reynolds rubbed his left arm. Again. "You're no better than your old man, are you?"

Joe cursed under his breath. It took all he had not to come clean, to blurt out the truth, just to shut Reynolds up. But he held fast to the promise he'd made Kristin, in spite of the urge to toss it aside.

Sweat dotted the older man's upper lip and brow as the redness of his suppressed fury slipped away, leaving a lifeless, gray color in its wake. He grimaced, and his face distorted in anger. Or was that pain?

"Are you okay?" Joe asked.

Instead of answering, Reynolds clutched his chest, then slumped to the ground.

"Jeffries! Garcia!" Joe called to the paramedics on duty. "Get over here quick!"

Joe dropped to his knees beside the prostrate man and felt for a pulse, listened for breathing and found neither.

He tilted Reynolds's head back, pinched his nose and covered his mouth with his own. Blow. Blow.

Nothing.

He placed his hands upon his chest, utilizing the training and skill that had become second nature, and hoped it wasn't too late. Pump. Pump. Pump…

Garcia was the first to arrive. "What have we got here?"

"Heart attack," Joe said. "I think."

Garcia and Jefferson took over, as Joe stood to the side and watched Kristin's father fight for his life.

He'd never liked the old man. But he didn't want to see him die. Not like this.

His mind drifted to Kristin, to his son. To the grief he knew they'd both suffer if they lost Thomas Reynolds.

Dennison pulled up in the paramedic unit, an emergency room on wheels.

"I'm going with you," Joe said.

Then, as they loaded an ashen-faced Reynolds into the ambulance, Joe climbed inside, feeling as helpless as a kid on a ride-along.

He knew better than to ask Garcia or Jeffries if the old man would make it. He'd seen enough to know the prognosis didn't look good.

Chapter Eleven

The ride to the hospital passed in a blur, as the paramedic unit raced through traffic.

Sirens roaring. Lights flashing. Defib zapping. Oxygen flowing. IV dripping.

Both Jeffries and Garcia worked steadily, trying to stabilize Thomas Reynolds, yet reviving the real estate baron appeared hopeless to Joe. Reynolds hadn't regained consciousness yet and his color was still a pasty gray.

When they pulled to a stop in front of the E.R. doors, the paramedics rushed the nearly lifeless shell of a man into the hospital. Joe followed the gurney until a nurse on staff shooed him out of the room. "I'm sorry, but you'll have to wait outside."

Joe knew the procedure, so he stepped aside. The dark-haired nurse closed the door and joined the cardiac triage crew as they worked to save the life of Kristin's father.

Oh, God. *Kristin.* She didn't know.

He blew out a sigh and raked a hand through his hair, knowing he should be the one to tell her, not some faceless voice claiming to be a hospital spokesman.

Of course, he wasn't keen on letting her know all the details, such as what her father had been doing when he suffered the heart attack. He spotted a pay phone near the E.R. restrooms and dug through his pocket for change as he approached. Then he dialed Kristin's number and waited.

After a couple of rings, a woman with the hint of an English accent answered—the maid, most likely—and told him Kristin wasn't home. He considered leaving a message, but decided against it. He'd try Kristin's cell phone first.

When she answered, he found it difficult to find the right words. "Kristin, it's Joe. Your father's at Oceana General Hospital. He had an apparent heart attack, and the paramedics brought him in. Can you meet me here?"

"Oh, my God. Yes. But it will take me at least thirty minutes to get through this traffic. I took my dad's SUV back to the dealership in San Diego." Her breath caught, and he knew she was holding back a sob. "Is he okay?"

"I'm not sure. The doctor is with him now."

She didn't respond right away, so in an attempt to not

feel so helpless, he told her, "The paramedics who worked on him are the best we have, and they got to him right away."

"That's good to know," she said, her voice soft. Tentative. "I'm glad you were on call when it happened. And that you were with the paramedics when they brought him in."

He hadn't gone out on a call. Her father had showed up at the fire department and blown a fuse. But Joe didn't correct her. Not now.

"Where's Bobby?" he asked.

"Here. In the car with me. Oh, gosh. Going back to the house is out of the way. And—"

"Just bring him to the hospital. I'll take care of him for you. He doesn't need to be hanging out in a place like this."

"Okay." She blew out a shaky sigh. "Thanks for calling, Joe. And for waiting for me there. I know how things have been in the past…and I appreciate…" She paused again, probably struggling with all the emotions she had to be dealing with.

"I'm here for you, Kristin. And for Bobby." He bit his bottom lip, holding back the rest of it. Their secret was out—in spite of her wishes. And Thomas Reynolds had reacted just as she'd suspected; he'd flown off the handle, and his heart couldn't take it.

"Thanks. I appreciate that. I'll hurry as fast as I can."

"Drive careful, honey." He paused in mid-breath when he realized he'd let the endearment slip out, as though they were more than friends. But maybe she hadn't even noticed. "I'll wait until you get here."

The line disconnected, and he took a seat next to a guy with a bloody towel wrapped around his hand and a kid with red, watery eyes and a nasty cough.

Why didn't someone on staff put the boy and his mom in a room by themselves? Half the E.R. was going to get sick. Or sicker.

Minutes passed, although he didn't know how many. Twenty? Thirty? Forty?

Why hadn't he looked at a clock after he'd made that call? Not that it mattered, he supposed. He'd already cleared things with the chief.

Each time the automatic double doors swung open, Joe looked up, hoping to see Kristin yet dreading the grief he knew would mar her pretty face and cloud those emerald eyes.

But finally, his glance was rewarded.

Kristin clutched Bobby's hand, as she rushed through the automatic glass door to the emergency room. She'd tried to calm her son on the way here, telling him not to worry when she was a practically a basket case herself.

But she wasn't ready to lose her father. Not now. And not when she had so many things to explain, to apologize for.

The sights and smells of the hospital accosted her, and she scanned the crowded waiting room. But she didn't have to look very long.

Joe stood and quickly made his way toward her. Just knowing she wasn't alone in all of this helped. And his support meant more than she could have guessed. It felt as though reinforcements had arrived and everything would be okay.

She tried to read his face, his expression, to determine whether her father was still alive, still holding on. Whether she and Bobby had any hope they could cling to.

As they met, Joe opened his arms, and she fell into his embrace, absorbing his comfort, relishing his scent. Her head rested against his cheek, and she clung to him. She'd always been affected by his touch, by his proximity, but this time it was different.

His support, both physical and emotional, gave her hope and warmed her heart, taking the edge off the chill of fear. Leaning on Joe felt so natural, so normal.

Too natural. *Too* normal.

She withdrew from his arms and tried to emotionally regroup. Joe was her son's father—not her husband. Not her lover. And his embrace had been offered as comfort. She didn't dare depend on any more than that from him. Yet she regretted the loss of his touch the minute she stood alone.

But she was determined to be self-reliant. "Do you know what happened? Where was he? What was he doing at the time?"

Joe didn't respond right away, and she had this weird feeling that he was trying to keep something from her. Like maybe her father was one of the unlucky men who'd had a heart attack while in bed with a mistress or a prostitute.

Her eyes widened, and her lips parted. Surely that wasn't the case.

"Your dad came by the station, Kristin. Looking for me."

Her heart thudded in her chest. "Why?"

"He knows, honey. And he wasn't happy about it."

"You told him?" Her voice, although she could have sworn the words came out in a whisper, seemed to shriek, to rage. "How could you? You upset him and sent him over the edge."

"That's not how it happened." Joe glanced down. In shame, she suspected. Until she realized he was looking at her son. *Their* son.

Bobby's bottom lip quivered, and his eyes filled with worry.

How could she snap like that at Joe while Bobby stood beside her, concerned about what might happen to his grandfather.

Kristin blew out a sigh, then knelt to his level. "I'm so sorry, Bobby. I'm a little scared, that's all. But Grandpa is here at the hospital now. And the doctors are working hard to make him better."

Joe knelt, too, joining her at their son's side. "This is one of the best hospitals in the state, sport. And I know for a fact they save a lot of people every day."

She took Bobby's hand in hers. "Joe offered to take you home for me, so I can discuss treatments and medication with Grandpa's doctors. That way, you won't need to wait here."

"Is Grandpa going to be okay?" Bobby asked.

"We'll both have to pray that he will be." She kissed her son goodbye, then mastered a smile for his sake.

Joe took Bobby by the hand, then cupped Kristin's cheek with the other. "Call me and keep me posted."

She nodded, then watched Joe lead their son outside, leaving her more alone, more frightened than she'd ever felt before. But she bolstered herself with a shot of courage to face the next few hours, whatever they might bring. And then she went to let the medical personnel know that Thomas Reynolds's daughter was here, waiting for word of her father's condition.

Bobby was pretty quiet on the ride home, which was okay with Joe. Sometimes a guy needed to think, to clear his head and get a handle on his feelings.

As they turned onto the street that led to Playa del Sol, Joe prodded him to speak. "Are you feeling okay?"

"Yeah."

"You're pretty quiet."

"I was praying for my grandpa."

Joe nodded.

"I asked God to make my grandpa all better."

"Good," Joe said. He wasn't sure how to deal with a kid's grief. He wasn't trained. Not like Dylan. And for a moment, he felt out of his league.

"Will you pray for my grandpa, too?" Bobby asked.

Joe nearly choked. *Him? Pray?* For Thomas Reynolds?

Hell, he and God hadn't been on speaking terms for years. And somehow, it didn't seem fitting for the first breach of silence to be over a bastard like Reynolds.

"I…uh…" He looked at his son. What the heck was he supposed to tell him? Think, Davenport, think. "I… uh…can't close my eyes. I'm driving. But you go ahead and pray for me."

"You don't have to close your eyes," Bobby said. "God doesn't care about that."

Joe slid a glance at his son. It wasn't that easy. A guy didn't just drop in on God and start asking for favors— even if the favors were for someone else.

Or did that matter? Maybe it might make it more acceptable.

Bobby looked at him with big puppy-dog eyes, wearing his vulnerable little heart on his sleeve, yet boasting a faith that was a heck of a lot stronger than Joe's.

Joe blew out a sigh of resignation. "Is it okay if I keep my eyes open and my mouth shut?"

"Sure."

Oh, brother.

He cleared his throat, even though he had no intention of uttering a word out loud, and gripped the steering wheel tight, even though he'd already parked in his driveway and shut off the engine.

How did a guy go about starting a prayer?

Now I lay me down to sleep came to mind. But that couldn't be right. Besides, Joe didn't know the rest of it.

The Lord is my shepherd. Nope, too generic.

He glanced at his son, afraid to ask the kid something so simple. When he caught Bobby's hope-filled gaze, he closed his eyes—more to shut out the boy than succumb to divine protocol.

All right, God. Here I am. And I don't know what to say. I don't ask much of you. I haven't since that time I asked you to heal my mom from the cancer and my old man from his drug problem. You didn't listen then, so I'm not sure if this request will get through. But I got a bigger problem now. See, this kid means the world to me. And even though his grandpa is a real son of a bitch...

Joe cleared his throat again, sneaked a peek at Bobby, then realized the kid couldn't read minds. Or prayers. Of course, he probably ought to be more concerned about using that kind of language with God. But hell, wasn't God supposed to hear, see and know everything?

He couldn't see any reason to sugarcoat feelings the Almighty had already tapped into. *Well, heck, God. You know what kind of man Reynolds is. And I figure, if he shows up at the Pearly Gates, you'll have someone in a white gown instruct him to make a U-turn. So you can see why I'm struggling with this request. But the fact is, I don't want the old guy to die. Not if it's going to hurt my son. And his mother.*

I probably don't deserve any favors from you. But could you find some time to step in and do something for Bobby and Kristin? Joe opened his eyes, saw that Bobby was watching him intently.

"Did you say Amen yet?" the boy asked.

Oops. *Amen.* Joe nodded, then for safe measure, added, *Thanks for your time, God. I'll owe you one if you take care of this for my son and his mom.*

Then he blew out a sigh—glad that was over. "Come on, Bobby, let's go inside."

As they approached the front door, Bobby's footsteps slowed. "Is my mom mad at you about something?"

He didn't know how to explain to Bobby that his mom thought Joe had caused his grandpa's heart attack. But that wasn't true. And even though it wasn't, he had a feeling she'd never forgive him for something that hadn't been his fault, something that had been out of his power to correct. But he wasn't about to tell his son that. "Your mom was pretty upset, and she lashed out at me. But she's worried about your Grandpa, so I understand."

"You're not mad at her?" Bobby asked.

"Nope."

Once inside, Bobby headed for the GameCube controllers that rested on the glass-top coffee table. "Want to play?"

"Sure."

They sat before the TV screen, but Joe had a hard time focusing on the game. Instead, he kept glancing at Bobby, making sure he was holding up all right.

Okay, so Bobby wasn't acting like the same happy-go-lucky kid he'd been in the past. But neither was he brooding or overly troubled. At least, it didn't seem that way to Joe.

Unable to keep his curiosity at bay, he decided to bring up the gloomy artwork. "I hear you drew a picture of you and me."

The boy nodded, a crooked smile breaking onto his face. "Yeah. Just like this. You and me sitting on the sofa with the game on TV."

"I'd like to see it someday."

Bobby nodded, as he jabbed at the yellow button on the controller in his hand. "Okay. But it would have looked a lot better if I had *my* crayons. Mrs. Davies took me to see her dumb niece who is a real brat and only gave me a black crayon to use. She wouldn't share any of her other crayons with me, just 'cause I'm a boy."

Black was the only color he had?

Joe sat back and leaned against the sofa. *Well, I'll be damned.* There was a simple explanation for something Dylan had made such a big, psychological fuss over.

And quite frankly, Joe felt a surge of pride knowing he had a better understanding of his kid's psyche than good ol' Dr. Dylan, superstar of the TV talk-show circuit.

In the past, Joe had let Thomas Reynolds convince him that he wasn't the kind of man Kristin needed. And more recently, he'd even fallen into the mistaken belief that Dylan was the kind of man she deserved.

But that wasn't true. She deserved a man who understood Bobby. A man who understood her.

A man like Joe Davenport.

Of course, Kristin didn't appear to be in the mood to handle a revelation like that. Not now. And maybe not ever.

Not while her father was fighting for his life in the hospital.

And not while she blamed Joe for it.

Kristin remained at the hospital throughout the night, as doctors tried to stabilize her father. She hadn't been able to read any of the magazines placed throughout the ICU waiting room, nor had she been able to watch the television that had been mounted on the wall in the corner.

A hundred memories flipped through her head in no particular order—Christmas mornings, horsey-back rides. Those faux-ruby-slipper shoes he'd bought her for Valentine's Day one year so she could look like Dorothy. He'd thought they looked gaudy and goofy, but he'd let her wear them all over town.

When she was finally allowed to go into ICU, she made her way to his bedside where he lay with eyes closed. Pale.

It killed her to see him like this, tied to the bed by wires and tubes and blinking machines.

"Hi, Daddy."

He didn't respond.

A nurse slipped up behind her. "He's been conscious, but the doctor gave him a sedative and he's resting pretty easy now."

Kristin nodded. She stroked his arm and rested her hand upon his fingers, then glanced at the nurse. "Do you know if they've scheduled the bypass surgery?"

"Not yet. But from what I understand, when Dr.

Nichols mentioned the procedure, your father refused to give his consent."

"Why?"

The nurse shrugged. "Maybe you can talk to him. Surgery is often frightening."

Her father wasn't frightened. He was stubborn. And she had to talk some sense into him, let him know that to refuse the surgery would hurt her. And since she hadn't had time to make peace with him, with the lies she'd told, his death would feel like an eternal punishment.

She closed her eyes and blew out a ragged breath. *A punishment.* It was funny, now that she thought about it, but he'd never punished her as a little girl for doing the usual childish pranks. But when she'd disappointed him, challenged his authority...

Was *that* what he was doing now? Holding his recovery over her head? A knot formed in her stomach as she realized that possibility. And yet another.

Was he no longer interested in living, in being the father of a young woman who'd been lying to him for years?

"You'll need to leave now," the nurse said. "But in an hour, you can come back."

Kristin nodded, then placed a kiss on her father's brow before letting the soft-spoken nurse lead her out of ICU. As she stepped into the hall, she recognized Dylan.

Bless his heart. He'd come to offer his support.

He opened his arms, and she fell into his steady embrace. He was every bit as tall and strong as Joe, and his scent, a wood-and-spice blend, was just as pleasing.

His comfort just as sincere. But being in his arms didn't feel as natural, as normal. As right.

She withdrew from his embrace, ashamed that she could compare the two men at a time like this.

"I can't stay long, sweetheart." Dylan gently brushed a strand of hair from her cheek. "I've got a meeting with the network execs this afternoon, but I wanted to be here for you."

"Thanks."

"How's your father doing?" he asked.

"I haven't talked to him yet. But from what the nurse said, he's refusing to give his consent for surgery."

"He's a smart man, honey. And with his health complications, he's probably weighing the risks."

It was more than that, and she knew it. But she kept her thoughts to herself. A tear slipped down her cheek, and she brushed it away with the length of her index finger.

Dylan took her hand. "Come on. Let's see if there's something we can do about his apprehension."

He led her to the cardiac wing, then to the nurse's desk, where an older RN with graying red hair sat.

"Excuse me," Dylan said. "Do you have anyone who can talk to Mr. Reynolds about his upcoming surgery? Someone who's been through a similar procedure?"

"As a matter of fact, we do." The nurse smiled. "We have a couple that often comes to the hospital at our request to speak to an apprehensive patient. And they've had remarkable success."

"Great," Dylan said. "Can you please ask them to visit with Mr. Reynolds?"

"I'd be happy to."

The nurse flipped through a Rolodex, withdrew a card, then quickly dialed. She smiled. "Hi, Kay. This is Helene down at Oceana General. We've got another patient in need of counseling. And his family wondered if you and Harry could come and talk with him about his surgery."

Kay and Harry? Kristin stiffened. The Logans counseled heart patients? Surely it was another couple.

Helene hung up the telephone. "They'll be here within an hour or two. If anyone can make a pre-op patient feel better about an upcoming bypass surgery, it's Harry and Kay Logan."

But what about *this* pre-op patient?

Kristin's knees wobbled like one of those little round-bottomed toys Bobby used to play with. Something told her a visit with Harry Logan would send her father over the edge.

And that the visit might do him more harm than good.

Chapter Twelve

Kristin didn't know how Dylan had done it. Or maybe it was Harry's clout at the hospital that made things happen so quickly. But two hours later, after Dylan had returned to L.A., she stood with Kay and Harry Logan at her father's bedside.

The retired detective talked to her dad about the success of his own bypass four months ago, in spite of similar complications. But Thomas Reynolds had merely glared at him.

"Do you have any questions or concerns about the surgery or recovery?" Harry asked.

"I've got a lot of questions and concerns," her father barked. "But none that I want to discuss with you, Logan."

"Still holding a grudge, I can see."

Her father turned his head toward a blinking screen that monitored his heartbeat, but Kristin doubted he gave a darn what the blips and blinks meant.

"It seems to me that it's time to put the past behind us. Don't you, Mr. Reynolds?"

Her father lay on the bed, unyielding, even in his weakness.

Harry cleared his throat. "Well, maybe it's best if I leave you with the ladies." He placed a hand on his wife's shoulder, as though passing the relay baton, then slipped out of the room.

Kay eased closer, taking her husband's place. "I'd like to pray with you, Mr. Reynolds, if that's all right."

Her father scowled. "Don't waste your breath. I believe in the *here and now,* not the hereafter."

Kay didn't bat an eye. "That's too bad. But without the bypass, you don't have much time left in the here and now."

His eye twitched. A sign that her words had broken through? Or merely an indication of the intensity of his resolve?

"It's time to get right with God and with the people you'll be leaving here on earth."

"Make things right?" Her father snorted, then rolled his eyes.

"Perhaps there are things that need to be said, amends that need to be made." Kay's voice bore a soft and kind edge, yet was filled with conviction.

"I've never done anything to be sorry for." Her father turned his head toward the monitor again.

This stubborn island of a man was a side she'd never seen of her father.

When had he become so hardened? So crass and egocentric? Had he always been that way and she'd never recognized it?

Well, he was showing that side of himself now.

"It's a funny thing about forgiveness," Kay said. "We often want our mistakes and sins to be overlooked, but we don't want to forgive others."

"You're wasting your time, Mrs. Logan. The old boy upstairs gave up on me a long time ago. And you'd be wise to do the same thing."

Kay seemed unaffected by her father's rudeness, but Kristin wasn't. It hurt to see him like this, and she refused to subject herself to any more of it.

Excusing herself, she left Kay at his bedside, but didn't have much hope of the soft-spoken woman getting through to him.

Her father had always had an aggressive attitude toward business. He had a need to succeed at all costs that drove him onward in spite of obstacles standing in his way. In the past, she'd found it admirable. But that was no longer the case.

She'd heard rumors about failed businesses of people who'd crossed him, but before today, she'd never believed them.

Apparently, she'd never really known her father. Not

the real man. And that fact, added to her fear of losing him, mingled with her guilt. Tears welled in her eyes, and she blinked them back.

Once outside the ICU, she joined Harry in the hall. "I'm really sorry about my father's attitude."

"Don't be. It's not your fault." Harry offered her a fatherly smile. The kind of smile she might never see again.

She tried to smile in return, but her heart couldn't quite muster the effort. "I appreciate you and Kay coming to talk to my dad today, even though he rejected everything you said or offered."

"Hey, it's something Kay and I like to do. Sometimes it helps, sometimes it doesn't. My wife sees it as a ministry of some kind. I just think of it as payback for being given a second chance at life."

Kristin turned toward the closed door, wondering if Kay would soon be dashing out with her tail between her legs, chased out by an unyielding man with a suicidal death wish of some kind.

Harry placed a gentle hand on her shoulder. "Don't worry yet. Your father is a hard man to reach. And he holds a grudge like a hungry bulldog grabs a bone. But if anyone can get through to him, it's my wife."

Kristin wasn't so sure.

But what Harry had said about her father was apparently true. He'd never gotten past the fire Joe had started when he was just a kid. Never gotten over the resentment and hate. And it was time that she faced the truth about him.

"I have a question I'd like to ask you," she said.

"Shoot."

"Are the rumors true about my dad? Did he try to ruin people who crossed him?"

"Thomas Reynolds hasn't endeared himself to many in the community. Including me."

"Can I ask why?"

"They're personal reasons."

"Does it have anything to do with that juvenile court incident when Joe was in trouble?"

Harry glanced down at his loafers, then caught her eye. "Your father took his anger a bit too far and has held a grudge for entirely too long."

"What do you mean?"

Distracted, he looked toward the ICU door. Kristin followed his gaze and watched as Kay exited.

The older woman didn't appear to be running scared. Or annoyed by the conversation she'd just had. She smiled, first at her husband, then at Kristin.

Was that an indication of a successful persuasion?

Kristin wouldn't know unless she asked. "How'd it go?"

"I'm not sure. Some people need to chew on things for a while before they can begin to digest what was said." The older woman slipped her hand in her husband's. "Time will tell. But if you need anything, just give us a call."

Kristin nodded, then watched the older couple walk away hand in hand.

How nice to have a partner in life, a lover, a best

friend. She glanced at the doorway of the ICU where her father lay, stubborn and unreachable.

He'd never done anything to be sorry for? That was hard to believe.

Or was he talking about his relationship with her?

In a way, she supposed he didn't owe her an apology. He'd never hurt her. Never lied. Never snuck behind *her* back.

Of course, she hadn't meant to hurt him, to deceive him. Her lies had been to protect Joe, to protect the love she harbored for a young man her father didn't approve of. And more recently, she'd lied to protect her father from his own anger.

But would he have been angrier with Joe for fathering Bobby, or with Kristin for disappointing him, for lying?

She blew out the breath she'd been holding. Who had she really been trying to protect?

The secret was out now. Did she dare stir the pot? Risk angering him more?

She glanced at the doorway to the ICU. Things certainly couldn't get much worse.

The next hour passed slowly. At five o'clock, a short, dark-haired nurse allowed Kristin entrance.

She made her way to his bedside and stood before the man who'd adored her, the man who'd loved her with his whole heart. The man who hadn't been around very much when she was a little girl, but who'd taken the baton after her mother died and done all he could to make life easy on a grieving child.

She tried to find the words to explain, to apologize. To make things right between them, when they might never be right again.

"Daddy?"

He stirred, then opened his eyes. But he didn't speak.

"I lied to you. And I'm sorry."

He looked at her, but didn't smile, didn't give any hint that he'd be willing to forgive her.

But she pressed on, determined to get the truth out in the open. "I fell in love with Joe Davenport years ago. And I continued to see him, even though you'd told me not to. And when he stopped loving me, it broke my heart. But I didn't tell him I was pregnant. He never knew."

Her father's eyes bore straight to her heart, into her conscience. "You're my daughter, and you lied to me."

"I was afraid you'd go after Joe, that you'd make life difficult for him, when he was trying his best to overcome a crummy childhood and a lousy father."

Her confession settled around her like a fog in a marsh. In a way, perhaps she'd always suspected her father would go after anyone who crossed him. Apparently, that was why he'd never liked Joe. But now Kristin was the one who'd challenged him. Deceived him.

Her dad didn't speak. He merely shot her a look of disappointment that ripped her in two.

A tear ran down his craggy cheek. Then he turned his head and faced the wall.

Shutting her out.

Rejecting her.

"Dad, I wish you would be more understanding."

No response.

"I've apologized, but I won't beg. You can accept it and we can go forward. Or not. It's your choice."

There was still no crack in the silent wall he'd reinforced by presenting his back. And, quite frankly, she was tired of banging her head.

"I feel very sorry for you, Daddy. Because I truly believe that if my mother hadn't died, you would have become a different man. A more forgiving man."

At the mention of her mother, he slowly rolled to the side. "You're probably right about that, Kristin. I did love her, in spite of what she might have thought. And God knows she was always harping on me about one thing or another, trying to make me into the kind of husband and father she thought I ought to be. But she's gone. And you and I were left to fend for ourselves in this world."

"And I let you down," she said.

He didn't nod, didn't need to.

"And there's no room in your heart for people who challenge you, is there?"

"That's about the size of it. If you want my forgiveness, you need to stop seeing Joe altogether. And you need to marry Dylan. Today. Tomorrow. As soon as it can be arranged."

A knot formed in Kristin's stomach. He was bartering with her. Negotiating. Making demands that she would need to meet in order to receive his forgiveness.

"I'm sorry, Daddy. But I won't marry Dylan. I don't love him. I love Joe. And even if Joe doesn't feel the same way about me, he'll always be in my life because of Bobby. And there's nothing you can do about that."

She waited for a response, but didn't expect one. And when the silence was nearly overwhelming, she turned and walked away, unable to do any more to change her father's mind.

And unwilling to bend to his demands.

Kristin remained in the waiting room for the rest of the evening, but didn't step foot into the ICU. If her father had a change of heart, which wasn't very likely, she was nearby. And if the doctors had reason to speak to her, they knew where to find her.

Her relationship with her dad had hit the skids, but that didn't mean she didn't love him, didn't fear losing him any more than she already had.

At eight-thirty, she called Joe. A part of her wanted to ask him to leave her son with his neighbor and come to the hospital to be with her. But it was too much to ask a man who had only offered her emotional support and friendship, and too little to accept when she wanted so much more from him.

She used the pay phone in the hall and dialed his number. When his baritone voice came over the line, a flood of emotion filled her heart and clogged her throat. But she didn't dare deal with the past, the present or the possibility of a future. Not now.

And at this point, her only concern was for her son. "Hi. How's Bobby doing?"

"He's fine. A little subdued, but hopeful."

"Good."

"For what it's worth, Bobby told me that the little girl he'd been visiting had only allowed him to use a black crayon, so that's why he'd drawn that picture without any colors."

"That's a relief. Dylan obviously jumped to the wrong conclusion." She paused, still unable to sort through her own thoughts, unable to determine how much—if anything—to reveal about what was weighing on her heart.

"How's your dad?" he asked, his voice rough yet gentle, his concern real.

"Hanging in there," she said, wanting to open up, to vent, to cry in frustration and pain. But Joe didn't need any extra ammo in the cold war he had with her father. And somewhere, deep inside, she still wished her dad would see reason, forgive her and give Joe a chance.

Still, there were some things that needed to be said. "My father's a stubborn man. And I think he'd rather die than open his heart to anyone right now. Especially to someone who hurt him."

"For what it's worth," Joe said, "I didn't tell him anything. He saw us together in town and came to his own conclusion."

If she would have been thinking clearly, she would have realized Joe was the kind of man who would keep his promise. "I'm sorry for lashing out at you. I was just so scared, so worried…about what would happen when he found out."

She supposed, if anyone was to blame, it was her.

"And how are *you* doing, Kristin?"

Her? She was struggling to face the rift between her and her father, a gaping chasm that had been built years ago and that she'd failed to acknowledge. Her lip quivered, and she feared her voice would falter, too. "I'll be all right."

And one way or another, she would be.

"If you need someone to be with you, I can leave Bobby with Chloe. She's really good with kids."

Before Kristin could actually contemplate the suggestion, she noticed Dylan striding down the hall. "I'm okay for the time being. Dylan just arrived."

Joe paused, then said, "That's good. I'm glad you're not alone. Don't worry about Bobby. I'm taking some family leave time, so I can keep him as long as you'd like me to."

"Thanks." She wasn't keen on breaking the connection, on losing the sound of Joe's voice, but the closer Dylan came, the more she felt like ending the call. "I'll have to talk to you later, okay?"

"Sure."

Kristin hung up the telephone and greeted Dylan. She should feel buoyed by his presence, but for some reason, his arrival was bittersweet.

"I rescheduled the filming of the morning show."

Dylan offered her a hug, which wasn't nearly as soothing as Joe's had been. And although she appreciated having his arms around her, it didn't lift her guilt, her worry, her loneliness.

It was Joe's embrace she wanted. Joe's support. Joe's love. And the reality sank to the pit of her heart.

"No matter what happens," Dylan said. "I want you to know I love you and I'm here for you."

The words should have helped, should have made her lean into him and hang on for dear life. But they didn't, and she withdrew from his embrace.

Dylan furrowed his brow. "What's the matter, Kristin?"

"I appreciate you coming, Dylan. And I value our friendship."

"Our friendship?" A look of disbelief crossed his face, as though he was shocked to know she'd meant what she'd told him before—that she wasn't ready to marry him.

Most women would be thrilled to have a man like Dylan for a husband. But in spite of Dylan's wisdom and perfection, Kristin didn't love him. Not the way she'd once loved Joe. Not the way she still loved Joe.

And she couldn't imagine spending the rest of her life with a man who didn't turn her heart inside out.

"I don't love you." The words surprised her, nearly as much as his expression suggested they'd surprised him. "At least, not in the right way. And I don't want you to have any sense of false hope. I won't marry you. I'm sorry."

He ran his hand through the hair that was always combed, always perfect, and mussed it in a way that made him look human. "I won't tell you that I'm okay with this. It hurts."

She almost uttered another apology, but bit her tongue. There wasn't any way to make this easy for him.

"It's Davenport, isn't it?"

Kristin nodded. "I've always been in love with my son's father. And returning to Bayside, seeing him again, watching him bond with Bobby, has only made me love him more."

"I suspected there was something going on between the two of you." Dylan cleared his throat, then shoved his hands in the pockets of his Versace slacks. "Does Joe love you, too?"

"I don't know. And it really doesn't matter. I'm not looking for a husband on the rebound. And even if I were, you don't deserve to be second choice."

He blew out a weary sigh. "You're right. If I can't be first in your life, then it's best if we end things."

They stood in silence for a while, out of respect for a relationship that died. Then Dylan reached out and cupped her cheek. "You ought to get some rest."

She smiled, then glanced down at the beige linen outfit she wore, the bagged-out, wrinkled slacks. "I will, as soon as I feel comfortable leaving here."

"Can I get you anything?"

"No. That's all right. I'll be okay."

And she would be all right—even if her father passed away.

And even if Joe's love for her had died years ago.

* * *

Kristin remained at the hospital throughout the night, but she didn't go into her father's room. She couldn't.

If he shut her out again, the painful image would darken every memory she'd ever held of him. As it was, she could tell herself he was sick, medicated. Not in his right mind.

But if he rejected her apology one more time, if he threw it back in her face again, she'd fall apart. Or fly off the handle. Maybe pitch a fit. Throw a bedpan across the room.

"Ms. Reynolds?"

She turned at the sound of the masculine voice and saw her father's primary physician standing in the doorway.

"Is he…?" She couldn't even finish the sentence. Was her father dead? Was he asking for her? Had his conscience stirred? Was he offering forgiveness without a price?

"We're getting your father ready for surgery," Dr. Capshaw said.

"Against his wishes?"

"No. He agreed to the bypass. He had a close call about an hour ago, and we finally got through to him. The risk of the surgery no longer outweighs the risk of doing nothing."

"Can I see him?"

"I'm afraid not. Once we had his consent, things started happening fast."

She nodded, not sure whether her father's attitude before bypass surgery would be improved or hindered by a visit from her.

Deciding not to focus on it either way, she called Joe to let him know what was going on.

Or maybe she just wanted to hear the rich timbre of his voice. To feel a connection, even if it was only over a telephone wire.

"Joe, it's me."

"How are you holding up?" he asked.

She appreciated his concern, since it didn't appear as though she had anyone in her corner, not since she ran Dylan off. God, how she wished she had a sister or brother, someone to help her carry the emotional load. Or better yet, she wished her mother were still alive.

"I'm doing all right," she told Joe. Although, if he were standing here and could see what lack of sleep had done to her, he wouldn't believe her. She ran a hand through her hair, trying to comb out the tangles.

"And your dad?" Joe asked.

"They took him into surgery. I can call you when he's out."

"You're not by yourself, are you?"

She clutched the receiver tight, wanting so badly to tell him to please come sit with her, hold her hand. Hold her up. But she couldn't do it. Couldn't let him know how vulnerable she was, how badly she wanted him. "Don't worry about me. Just take care of Bobby."

"You know I will."

Then she sat down to wait.

Alone.

Chapter Thirteen

The next few hours passed slowly. Kristin had tried to get some rest, but never could relax, never could let go.

Several others waited in the same room—an older couple watching a game show on television, two young men in the far corner. But Kristin had no one. Just herself.

So, there'd been plenty of time to think, time to contemplate what she wanted out of life. What she needed. What she'd lost.

Throughout the morning, she'd wanted to pick up the phone and call Joe, to tell him she needed his support, his shoulder to lean on, his arms to hold her.

And that she needed his love.

But an admission like that would leave her open, vulnerable.

What if he didn't love her? And if he did, what if he walked out on her again? What if he broke her heart for a second time?

And even more unsettling—if Joe rejected her, how would that affect Bobby?

The murmurs and movements within the waiting room ceased when a doctor dressed in surgery scrubs entered. He strode toward Kristin. "Ms. Reynolds?"

"Yes." She stood.

"I'm Dr. Alvarado, the cardiovascular surgeon who performed the bypass on your father."

Her knees nearly gave out, but more from exhaustion than anything. "How is he?"

"He survived the operation and is doing as well as can be expected. The heart attack did some damage, but not nearly as much as it would have had he not received immediate attention. We'll have to wait and see how he does over the next few days, but let's say I'm cautiously optimistic."

She nodded, trying to take it all in. She was glad her dad's chances of making it had improved. Glad that the paramedics had been on hand when the heart attack had occurred. If her father had been at home or the office at the time, he might not have fared as well.

"It will be a while before your father can have visitors, so why don't you get some rest. If you let us know where to reach you, we'll keep you updated."

"Certainly." Her first thought was to leave her father's home number, but reconsidered. For some reason, she didn't think being in the family home would provide her the peace she needed to get some rest, especially since she hadn't been sleeping very well prior to the all-night vigil she'd spent in a chair in the ICU waiting room.

There was no place more restful than the historic mountain community of Julian. The quaint cabin had always seemed more like home to her than the house in which she'd grown up. Probably because it reminded her so much of her mother, a woman who'd been able to fix things with a smile and a hug. But it was too far away if she needed to rush back to the hospital for any reason. Maybe the Bayside Inn would be better.

"I'm not sure where I'll end up, Doctor. Can you call my cell phone?"

"Of course. Leave the number with Karen at the patient advocate's office."

"All right. I will." She reached for her purse and left the room, eager to be on her way. But before going anywhere, she would stop by Joe's and see about Bobby.

Twenty minutes later, she parked in a visitor space and glanced in the rearview mirror. When she saw her worn, frazzled image, she nearly changed her mind. She didn't want either Joe or Bobby to see her looking like something the cat had dragged in.

But Kristin wouldn't hide the truth any longer. She was bone tired. And emotionally exhausted. Only a fool would pretend the past twenty-four hours hadn't taken a toll on her.

She almost slapped on a coat of lipstick, but didn't think it would make any significant difference in her appearance. And she wasn't sure it even mattered. Right now, romance was at the very bottom of her priority list.

If she'd harbored any fantasies of Joe falling in love with her all over again, it certainly wasn't going to happen today. Not with her looking like a shipwrecked socialite who'd weathered a typhoon or two.

She climbed from the car, made her way to the porch and rang the bell.

Bobby answered and grinned from ear to ear, his eyes glistening. "Mom! You're back." Then he wrapped his arms around her waist. "How's Grandpa?"

"He's doing okay." Kristin held her son tight, but her eyes drifted to the tall figure standing behind him. The broad-shouldered, blond Adonis in worn jeans and a white T-shirt.

The first—and only—man she'd ever loved.

With sun-kissed hair, topaz eyes and a dimpled grin that could turn a woman inside out, he was a welcome sight for weary eyes. He looked so fresh. So robust. So utterly handsome, that she couldn't help but stare. Couldn't help but fall into the stunning depths of his amber gaze.

His thumbs were hooked into the front pockets of his jeans, but he caressed her just the same—with his eyes. "You said your father was doing all right. But how about you?"

Again, his concern was touching. Normally, she might have stood tall, told him she was fine. But it didn't take a Mensa candidate to see how frazzled she was.

She blew out a weary sigh. "Other than catnaps, I haven't slept in days. And I need a bath." She ran a hand through her hair, her fingers snagging in the tangles. "But I'll be okay after a soak in the tub and visit with the sandman."

"Did you want to take Bobby home?"

"I suppose so. But I'm not going home. I thought about driving to the Bayside Inn. Being at my father's house right now isn't all that appealing. And I'm not sure why."

"If you want, you can stay here." He nodded toward the bedroom. "Bobby and I were going to run some errands, so it'll be quiet."

"Maybe. I don't know." She swayed again, like a drunken sailor on the first shore leave in months. Maybe driving anywhere wasn't a good idea until she napped.

Joe took her by the arm and placed a supportive hand on her back. "You're not really okay, are you?"

She bit her lip, not sure how to ask for a hug. Not sure she wanted to reveal her need for one, but wanting his embrace so badly, it didn't seem to matter. "Can you hold me for a moment?"

"Sure." He slipped his arms around her waist and pulled her close.

She rested her head against his shoulder. His cologne, something sea-captain fresh and musky, snagged hold of her, offering more than comfort, more than strength.

In the past, she might have pulled away, tried to free herself from the snare of his embrace. But today, she held on for dear life.

They stood on his front porch in broad daylight, where all the world—or at least his neighbors—could see. But he didn't seem to mind.

His hands stroked her back—not in a sexual manner, but in a warm and loving way that offered her hope. Peace. Security. All the things she'd been missing lately.

Or maybe she was just rheumy from lack of sleep and unable to realize what she'd been missing. But either way, she seemed to have found it all in Joe's warm embrace.

Joe held Kristin, offering her all he was free to give. In his arms, she felt fragile, yet determined. And he suspected she'd needed this hug yesterday, as well as some hand-holding throughout the hospital ordeal. He would have sat with her, but she'd declined. She hadn't needed him.

"Where's Dylan?" he asked. "Has he been with you?"

"No. I sent him home yesterday."

"Why?"

Her hold loosened, but she didn't pull away. "I… uh…told him I didn't love him. And that I wasn't going to marry him."

The news sent his heart into a soaring loop-the-loop,

and he felt as though he'd just hit a home run with the bases loaded.

Dylan was out of the picture. That was great. But not just because his son wouldn't have the guy as a stepfather. Somewhere, in some irrational part of his mind, Joe actually liked the idea of Kristin being unattached. In fact, it made him want to try and re-stake his claim.

And why not?

She'd loved him once. Maybe she could love him again. And if so, maybe they could salvage the innocent dreams they'd once shared, create the kind of family their son deserved.

Of course, they'd have to tell Thomas Reynolds to take a flying leap if he tried to interfere. But Joe doubted Kristin would want to upset her dad, especially after nearly losing him. So that meant they were back to square one.

She slowly pulled away, leaving his arms empty. "Thanks, Joe. You have no idea how much I needed that."

"No problem." It had been his pleasure.

The classy woman who'd always dressed meticulously now sported a rumpled linen jacket and slacks. Even her string of pearls seemed to hang limp. And if she didn't appear to be so bedraggled emotionally, he'd think she looked cute. Lovable. Like a real woman who was actually attainable.

A woman who might take a chance on loving him again.

An admission of love lingered in his throat, but he

didn't dare open his heart and lay it on the line. Not now. Not until he had some idea how she felt about him. No need to spill his heart until he knew she wouldn't step on it.

"Come on inside," he said. "You can take a shower or bath here, if you'd like. And I'll give you one of my shirts to sleep in. Bobby and I will take off so it'll be quiet."

Nodding, she followed him into his living room, where the four walls seemed to light up, to perk up, just by her presence. His heart seemed to lighten, too.

And he wasn't sure whether that was a good thing or not.

Kristin woke to the sound of her cell phone ringing. For a moment, she didn't know where she was.

But she could smell Joe's scent in the sheets of his bed, and it all came back to her.

She rolled over, snatched the phone from the nightstand and flipped it open. "Hello?"

"Kristin Reynolds?"

"Yes." She fumbled for the switch on the lamp, until the light came on, then grimaced at the strain it put on her eyes.

"This is Marianne Boswell from Oceana General, one of the nurses in the ICU."

Uh-oh. Was something wrong? "How's my father?"

"Pretty feisty for a man who just came out of surgery. But he insists on talking to you, so I'm helping to put the call through."

Kristin clutched the small phone, pressing it closer to her ear.

"Krissy?" Her father's voice was hoarse and raspy, but the fact he'd used her childhood nickname offered a rush of hope.

"I'm here, Daddy."

"Honey, I want you to know I'm sorry. For so many things."

Oh, thank God. He wasn't going to hate her for the rest of his life, wasn't going to punish her. "Me, too, Daddy."

He cleared his throat, as though talking was an effort. Or maybe he was struggling to find the right words. "I've had a lot of time to think about what I've done. About what Harry's wife said to me. And the fact is, I want to make things right. And that's something I want to do, whether I live or die."

"I want that, too, Daddy."

"Good." He took a ragged breath, then slowly blew it out. "I've been trying to make decisions for you that weren't mine to make. And I made it so tough to challenge me, that you lied rather than buckle under my demands. I'm not going to fault you for that. It's your life, baby girl, and I'll try to respect your choices."

"I should have been honest with you, even if it caused a confrontation."

He paused for a moment, and she wondered whether he'd heard her, or if he'd succumbed to the effects of medication and dozed off. "I…uh…have some things to…confess…things I'm sorry for."

Each of his words seemed to be a struggle, and Kristin heard murmurs on the other line. The nurse, she assumed, was trying to take the phone away from him.

"Get the hell away," he muttered. "I'm sorry, Marianne. That was rude of me." He cleared his throat. "This turning-over-a-new-leaf business isn't as easy as it seems. Please, nurse. Just give me a minute more."

A new leaf? Was Thomas Reynolds actually admitting he needed to change? To bend?

Kristin wasn't sure what Kay had told him, but she'd said he would need to chew on her words for a while. And, apparently, he had.

"I want to get some things off my chest."

"What kind of things?"

He blew out a sigh. "Your mother wasn't happily married to me. And she'd asked for a divorce just before she died."

"Why?"

"She wanted more of my time, more of me. But I was too busy building a fortune to give her what she wanted. And too damn stubborn to apologize or try and make things right." He paused for a moment, as though trying to find the strength. "I might not have spent much time with her, but I loved her. And when she told me she'd become interested in someone else and was leaving and taking you with her, I did everything I could to prevent it. Everything except tell her the things that might have made her want to stay."

"What did you do?"

"I was furious. And hurt. And I lashed out at her, accusing her of infidelity when things probably hadn't gotten that far yet. And I began a custody battle I had every intention of winning—at any cost." He cleared his throat and choked out a little cough. "I should have taken time off work, taken her to Europe on a second honeymoon. Bought her roses everyday. Told her I loved her."

"I'm sure she knows how you feel now."

"I hope you're right. But I've been a bastard over the years. And I'm not sure that I deserve anyone's forgiveness."

"You have mine, Daddy."

"Thanks, but I haven't told you everything yet. I lied to you, too, Krissy."

"When?"

"Back when you asked me not to talk to Joe. I went to see him anyway and demanded he leave you alone. And when he refused, I offered him money. Five grand, to be exact. But he turned it down, and I had to try another tack. I convinced him that you deserved so much better than him."

Her father had instigated their breakup?

"Joe said he didn't love me anymore," she said, trying to grasp what had really happened eight years ago.

"I told him that if he really loved you, he'd let you go. And he did. I'm sorry for interfering. He's turned out to be a decent sort. And he's been good to Bobby."

"Yes, he's been wonderful." She nibbled on her bottom lip. Joe loved her back then? Did he still love her?

"Krissy, will you give a stubborn old man one more chance?"

She ought to be angry, unforgiving. But it was time to bury the past. To start living in the future. "Of course, Daddy. I'll come by in the morning and talk to you. Get some rest, all right?"

"Okay. I love you, baby girl."

"I love you, too."

She heard him mumble a thank-you to the nurse before the line disconnected.

There were some changes coming down the pike. Changes that would be interesting to watch unfold.

Kristin peered through the slats of the blinds into the darkened complex.

How long had she slept? Covering a yawn with her hand, she searched for a clock, but didn't spot one. Hadn't there been one in here earlier?

She swung her legs from the bed, but didn't stand. Instead, she reached for one of the pillows and held it under her nose, felt the softness that supported Joe's head, inhaled the musky scent that had provided her with his comfort during slumber.

It was a comfort she could grow to appreciate, if given the chance. After savoring one last whiff, she replaced the pillow near the headboard.

What time was it?

There was only one way to find out. She slipped out of bed, opened the bedroom door and padded into the living room. Her gaze fell on Joe, who sat on the sofa.

He wore a pair of worn jeans, unbuttoned at the top. No shirt. No shoes.

His lips quirked into a slow grin that stole her breath away.

"How'd you sleep?" he asked.

"Great. I think. What time is it?"

"Nearly midnight." He nodded toward the alarm clock on the lamp table. "I thought if you couldn't see the time, you might sleep better."

"It must have worked. I slept for about twelve hours."

"Yeah, well, we stayed away for most of the afternoon and evening, just so it would be more quiet."

That was sweet of him. "Thanks."

"I hope that call you received wasn't bad news."

"No. It was good. My father wanted to talk to me, to apologize about a few things. He's never been one to admit his mistakes, so it's nice to think we might be able to get things cleared up between us."

Joe nodded.

"Is Bobby asleep?"

"Yeah. Since about nine." He pointed toward a plastic bag on the recliner. "We picked up some things for you. A toothbrush. Some soap that Bobby thought would smell better to you than the stuff I use. The nightgown was Bobby's idea. He said you never sleep in things that show your legs and arms."

She didn't know why her son had come to that conclusion. She didn't always cover up like he'd implied, although she never wore skimpy nightclothes.

And speaking of skimpy, she glanced down at the front of the navy blue T-shirt that said Property of Bayside Fire Department and barely reached her thighs. She tugged at the hem, hoping it covered her panties.

"The nightgown we bought is kind of fancy and looks a lot like one Doris Day might have worn in one of those old movies, but it's long and has sleeves. Personally, I think the shirt looks better."

She smiled, her heart warmed by the compliment. But for some reason, she didn't want to be covered in satin from neck to ankles. Maybe because the spark of interest in his eyes pleased her, excited her.

But that would remain her secret. She glanced at the shopping bag. She'd already purchased a toothbrush while at the hospital, along with a travel-size tube of toothpaste, but didn't say anything. Nor did she mention that the soap she'd used in the shower earlier today wasn't so bad. In fact, the masculine, sea-breezy scent reminded her of him as she slid the bar over her slick, wet body.

"Do you want to look in on Bobby?" he asked. "I've given him the spare room and ordered him a bed, but they won't be delivering it until next Thursday. So we opened up the sofa sleeper."

Joe was making room for Bobby in his home, as well as his life. It was obvious he loved their son, which was great.

But could he love her again, too?

"Come on." Joe led her to the bedroom he'd given

Bobby and opened the door. Their son slept soundly, a blue plaid blanket draped over him, his arm clutching a brand new baseball mitt.

Apparently, Kristin wasn't the only one who'd benefited from the shopping trip.

"This room is still kind of cluttered," Joe whispered, "but I'm going to move some of this stuff to the storage shed, and Bobby's going to help me decorate it so it's more suitable for a kid."

The sofa bed took up most of the space, but a file cabinet rested in the corner, next to a set of golf clubs, a surfboard and a table that held a thirteen-inch TV.

Kristin suspected Bobby would enjoy fixing up the room that would be his. Apparently, he and Joe had discussed him visiting more often.

"Have you told him who you are?" she asked softly, no longer willing to hold Joe to his promise. What was the use?

"No. I promised to wait until you decided it was time. Remember?"

She did. And she appreciated Joe being a man of his word.

"And when the time is right," Joe added quietly. "I think it's something we should tell him together."

If there'd ever been a doubt about Joe's true colors, the truth shined through like a rainbow after a storm.

"You're right," she said. "And it's time to tell Bobby the truth. My dad has accepted the fact, but even if he hadn't, Bobby needs to know you're his father."

"Thanks."

They stood like that for a while, caught in a warm sense of family, as they watched their son sleep.

But Kristin was also accosted by sexual awareness, as sea-breezy whisper settled around her. Joe's presence was so real, so strong, that she could practically feel the warmth of his breath and the steady beat of his heart.

She wanted to turn, to wrap her arms around his neck and tell him that she loved him, that she'd never stopped. That she never would.

But a revelation like that might ruin the friendship they'd created for their son's benefit.

Still, a growing arousal continued to build, and she couldn't help but wonder whether he felt it, too.

She turned and caught his eye. Something brewed in the amber depths. Something she didn't dare try to interpret for fear she'd read something in it, something she wanted so badly to see.

He reached up, stroked the sleep-ruffled strands of her hair, but she didn't flinch. Didn't balk. She wanted him to touch her. To connect with her on some level. Any level.

Memories and unfulfilled dreams stirred between them as surely as if she and Joe had voiced each one out loud.

And God help her, she desperately wanted to relive every sweet moment they'd ever shared.

All she had to do was make the first move.

Joe had promised himself he wouldn't push Kristin, wouldn't ask for more than she was able to give. But she looked so damn sexy standing before him, her hair tousled from sleep and wearing nothing more than an old T-shirt that was destined to become his favorite.

As the pheromones and memories swirled around them, tangling them in something the years hadn't weakened, he decided to throw caution to the wind. "Did you ever love Dylan?"

"No," she said, her voice soft and velvety, like the lining of a jewelry box that held something valuable locked away. "I wanted to."

Joe couldn't help but poke at the lock, hoping it would open. "Why?"

"Because I wanted Bobby to have a two-parent family." The longing in her gaze turned his heart on end. "But no matter how kind he was to me and no matter how hard I tried, I could never really love him back. I love someone else, Joe. I always have. And I'm afraid I always will."

"Who?" he asked, still poking, still prodding. But he had to hear it. Had to be sure.

"I love *you*. But I'll try to put that aside for Bobby's sake."

Put it aside? God, his heart was pumping like a runaway train.

Kristin still loved him.

And he was struck by another grand-slam high. "Don't you think loving me will make things better for Bobby?"

"Not if you aren't able to love me again. Like you did once before."

Joe placed a hand along her jaw and stroked her cheek with his thumb. "I never stopped loving you, Kristin. Not ever. I just wanted to set you free. To give you a chance to meet a guy like Dylan. A guy who could give you the kind of life you deserved."

He didn't mention her father's involvement in that decision; he couldn't see any reason to. Joe could have told the old man to go to hell and continued to see her. But he hadn't. He'd let her go instead. And he would take full responsibility for the choice he'd made.

"Dylan couldn't possibly give me the kind of life I want," she said, her voice soft yet nearly breathless, "the kind of home and family I need."

A sappy grin that began in his chest busted free and rose to the surface. "Do you think I have a shot at giving you what you want and need?"

"You're the only one who can." The love in her smile drew him into her heart, her soul. "So what are we going to do about this, Joe?"

"We're going to do what we should have done years ago. We're going to get married and give our son a family."

She slipped her arms around his neck and dazzled him with a dimpled smile. "I'd like that. Very much."

"Oh yeah?" He slid her a crooked grin. "Then let's celebrate our engagement."

"What do you have in mind?"

"I can go to the liquor store down the street and buy a bottle of champagne—if you'll drink it with me in bed."

A playful grin lit her eyes. "I'm not willing to let you leave tonight, not even for a few minutes. But I'm all for celebrating. In bed."

Then she drew his mouth to hers. They kissed with youthful abandon, falling under the spell of the desire that had once consumed them, the fiery passion that promised to blaze for the rest of their lives.

She opened her mouth and their tongues mated, seeking and tasting, until they were consumed by the desire they'd once shared.

It took all Joe had to end the kiss, to nod toward the sleeping form of their son. "Come on. Let's take this into the other room."

"Good idea." She slipped her hand in his, fingers threading, linking them. Locking them together.

He led her into his bedroom, then closed the door, eager to make her his in every sense of the word. But when he turned and saw her waiting by the bed, his breath caught.

Wearing not much more than the navy-blue T-shirt, and sporting a shy but willing smile, she looked like a dream come true. His dream.

Ever so slowly, she lifted the hem of the shirt over her head, revealing a pair of white panties and breasts that were fuller, softer than he'd remembered. Breasts that he never thought he'd see again.

"Kristin," he whispered, his voice low, husky and filled with reverence. "You're beautiful."

She tucked a strand of hair behind her ear and

scrunched her pretty face. "You must not be looking at my stretch marks or the flabby pooch of my tummy."

He made his way toward her and placed a hand on her belly, on the faint lines that bore testimony of her pregnancy, of the child she'd carried for him. Then he dropped to his knees and kissed each mark.

Kristin's breath caught as he nuzzled lower, taunting her with his lips, his tongue. And when she thought her knees would surely buckle, he stood, lifted her in his arms and carried her to his bed, where he slipped off her panties and finished what he'd begun.

He kissed her where she'd never been kissed, loved her in a way she'd never been loved.

Feeling young and virginal again, she closed her eyes, enjoying every tantalizing sensation, arching toward him until she peaked and cried out when a powerful climax rocked her to the core.

When she opened her eyes, she saw him watching her with love glistening in his gaze.

"That was...wonderful. I've never...uh..." Well, she'd never experienced anything like that before. Read about it, of course. "It always seemed so...intimate. But with you, it was...natural and right."

He slid her a bad-boy grin, then rolled to the side, slipped off his jeans and took her into his arms.

Her breasts pressed against his chest, and he covered her mouth with his. Their hands caressed, explored, laying claim to each other's bodies.

As an ache grew deep in her womb, she reached for

him, letting him know she wanted him inside of her, where he belonged.

A moan sounded low in his throat, mingling with a whimper of her own. And when she didn't think she could stand it any longer, he entered her, making them one.

She met each of his thrusts, giving and taking until a star-spinning climax rocked her heart and soul.

They made love three times that evening, each sweet joining better than the last.

And as the sun slowly rose in the east, lighting the room and bringing the dawn of a new day, Joe ran a hand along the curve of her hip. "Your dad may have a hard time with this relationship."

"Daddy loves one Davenport kid. I'm sure he'll adjust to having another in the family."

"And if he doesn't?"

"You're going to be a priority in my life, Joe, along with Bobby. And my father will have to get used to that."

Then she brushed a kiss across his lips, a kiss that promised a unity they'd never had and a future they deserved.

When Bobby woke up, they would share the news with their son.

His grandfather would live.

And his mom was going to marry his dad.

Epilogue

Dressed in a classic-styled, ivory-colored wedding gown that had belonged to her mother, Kristin stood before the full-length mirror in her old bedroom. A fairy-tale princess stared back at her.

In just a few moments, she would marry Joe Davenport in an outdoor wedding at her father's house. And thanks to Kay Logan, who was proving to be a family friend, everything was storybook perfect.

Of course, it would have been nice to have her mother here. There were a few moments in Kristin's life when she really missed not having her mom. And this was one of them.

A light rap sounded at the door.

"It's me," her father said. "Are you ready?"

Kristin let him in and smiled. He looked dapper in the brand new tux he'd bought especially for the wedding. In fact, he looked so much healthier since his surgery just a month ago. Or maybe it was the new attitude that softened his expression, his smile.

He brushed a kiss on her cheek. "You look lovely, baby girl. Your mother would have been proud to see you in her dress." The glimmer in his eye faded a tad, and she suspected he missed her mother, too. More than he'd ever let on.

Kristin smiled, hoping to dislodge some of her father's sadness. "I like to think she's looking through a heavenly peephole."

"I hope so. Shall we go?"

She nodded.

Her father followed her down the stairs, then escorted her through the family room to the sliding door that led to the park-like backyard. Peering through the glass, she spotted the smiling crowd that had gathered to witness the ceremony and wish the newlyweds well.

The Logans sat in the front row of the side designated for the groom's family, taking the place of Joe's parents. And the guys from the station had nearly filled the other seats.

Kristin watched Chloe, who wore a dazzling red dress with a low-cut neckline, walk down the aisle on the arm of an off-duty fireman who was having a tough time keeping his eyes off the buxom redhead. Joe promised Kristin that she would like the woman, in spite of her flashy wardrobe. And Kristin was determined to give it a try.

A flower-adorned gazebo rested in the center of the lawn, surrounded by a colorful splatter of flowers from the gardens. There, Joe and Bobby stood by Reverend Morton of the Park Avenue Community Church.

Kristin and Joe had decided to forgo the usual bridal attendants, wanting only their son to stand at their sides.

The silver-haired woman who'd been hired to play the harp looked at Kristin and raised her brows, as though asking whether she should start the wedding march.

Kristin nodded.

As the chords of the familiar melody began to fill the air, her father placed a kiss on her cheek, then lowered the veil to cover her face. "I love you, Krissy."

"I love you, too, Daddy."

"Then let's get this show on the road. I'm hankering to be a grandpa again, so I hope you and Joe will hurry up and have another baby. That little Davenport boy needs a sister."

"We'll see if that can be arranged." Then she took his arm and gave it a squeeze.

As they made their way to the gazebo and she saw the man and child she loved waiting, her heart filled to the point of overflowing.

The sunshine glistened off the gold in Joe's hair, and his smile bore testimony of his love for her.

Her father handed her over to the man who would

soon be her husband, then took his seat in the front row, across from Harry and Kay.

The ceremony was simple and to the point. And before long, Reverend Morton pronounced Joe Davenport and Kristin Reynolds husband and wife.

Joe took her into his arms, sealing their vows with a kiss that promised forever.

And as they reluctantly pulled apart, Bobby gave out an ecstatic yell. "All right! Now we're a *real* family!"

The audience broke into laughter and applause.

"I'd like to second that emotion," Joe whispered to Kristin. "Come on, let's get the celebration under way."

Joe took one of Bobby's hands, and Kristin took the other, as they proceeded down the aisle together.

Man, wife and son.

"So far, our wedding day has been fairy-tale perfect," Kristin told her husband.

"You've got that right, honey." Joe gave her a wink. "And our happy-ever-after has only just begun."

* * * * *

*Don't miss the next story in
Judy Duarte's miniseries,*
BAYSIDE BACHELORS!

Turn the page for a sneak peek at
WORTH FIGHTING FOR (SE #1684)

Available May 2005.
Only from Silhouette Special Edition

Chapter One

Lieutenant Brett Tanner had never done anything so stupid.

Not since he'd joined the Navy ten years ago.

And he damn sure didn't know why he did it now, after all this time. Curiosity, he supposed, but for some reason he felt compelled to drive by the old house, to peer from a safe distance. To make sure his kid was okay.

He rode his black Harley Softail past the old high school, where he'd first met Kelly, his son's mother, and turned left at the fire station. The old neighborhood appeared the same, but he knew better.

The bike made another left onto Periwinkle Court, as though it didn't need a rider, then slowed to a stop.

Brett cut the engine before he reached the cul-de-sac, where the two-story house stood in silent testimony to the things that had remained the same.

And the things that hadn't.

The outside walls boasted creamy-white stucco. And the wood trim was painted a pale teal—something Kelly had repeatedly told him had needed to be done. Something he'd never gotten around to, since he'd been deployed most of the short time they'd been together.

For a moment, he had a masochistic urge to leave the Harley parked at the curb and saunter up the sidewalk as if he still owned the place.

But he remained rooted to the spot.

On a couple occasions, he'd reconsidered his decision to walk away from his son without a fight. But that was only after having one too many beers. When he was thinking clearly, he knew he'd done the right thing.

His son, a little boy Brett hadn't seen since he was two, deserved to be happy.

Why confuse the poor kid and screw him up now? Too much time had passed, and David Hopkins was the only dad Justin had ever known.

Besides, with the duty Brett pulled, he'd be in and out of the kid's life as if he were pushing through a revolving door. What good was that?

Brett didn't know how long he studied the house, the new fence, the bright yellow swing set in the backyard. But he stood there long enough to see that it was just the kind of home every kid ought to have.

It was vivid proof of all that was right in his son's world—now that Brett was no longer a part of it.

But Brett wasn't a deadbeat dad. The Navy deducted an allotment from his pay for child support. And each month, he sent Kelly a personal check for an extra two hundred dollars. For incidentals. Stuff his kid might need. Something a dad ought to provide.

It was also a way to keep in touch, to let Kelly know where he was—in case his son needed him. In case she wanted to send him a picture or something.

She hadn't sent him squat, not even a thank-you. But he hadn't pressed her, even though something deep inside fought his passive reaction.

Instead, he'd taken out an additional $250,000 life insurance policy—above and beyond what the Navy would provide his son—should something happen to him.

It had been his way of doing right by the kid he'd fathered.

And so had his letting go, staying away and allowing his child to grow up in a loving, peaceful home. Little Justin had two people who could be civil to one another. It was bound to be a hell of a lot better childhood than Brett had suffered through.

Just then, a little boy wearing a pair of jeans, a white T-shirt and a red baseball cap came out of the neighbor's side yard, ran a short distance down the sidewalk, leaped over a small hedge in the front of the house Brett had been watching, then dashed inside yelling, "Mom, I'm home."

That was his son. Justin.

Emotion clogged his throat, and his eyes went misty at the thought of what he'd given up.

He'd made the biggest sacrifice he would ever make. And time hadn't done a damn thing about easing the grief.

The same familiar ache settled deep in his chest, and his eyes began to water. Damn. He felt like bawling. And he hadn't cried in years. Not after he'd grown battle-weary and lashed out at his warring parents in a fit of rebellion that damn near landed him in jail.

Brett started the engine and turned the Harley around. It was time to head back to Bayside. Back to the condo he was house sitting for a Navy buddy. Back to a big-screen TV, a fridge full of beer and a crotchety old cat named Fred.

But his mind remained on the vision he'd seen, his son's perfect life.

Brett's parents' nasty divorce and vicious custody battle had lasted most of his growing up years and done a real number on him. For that reason, he'd sworn never to do that to a child of his own.

"I'd walk away first," he'd told Kelly, "rather than make my son a pawn, make him suffer like I did."

And Brett had kept his word—even though it nearly killed him not to be a part of Justin's life.

At the stop sign, he gunned the engine, then headed back to the condominium complex where he would spend his shore duty. But his chest still ached and his eyes stung.

What the hell was the matter with him?

Brett Tanner didn't cry. He sucked it up and did his duty. He did the right thing.

After all, he'd chosen the wrong road too many times in the past.

As tears welled in his eyes, he cursed the evidence of his weakness, then tried to lose the pain and anger as he sped through the city streets. He turned in the Ocean Breeze complex just as a white Volvo appeared from nowhere.

A loud metallic thud sounded when his bike slammed into the car. His body flew through the air, then slid along the driveway.

He didn't feel any pain at first. Not until his head cleared and he felt the sting of asphalt on his knees and arm, followed by an agonizing ache where his shoulder had hit the ground first.

The impact had sent his two-hundred-dollar sunglasses flying, probably smashing them to smithereens.

How was he going to explain this to the other driver? Or to a police officer, if one showed up on the scene? Or to any of his buddies, if they ever caught wind of this?

He'd had his head up his ass, thinking about his son. About the raw pain in his chest and the tears that clouded his sight.

And he'd caused an accident.

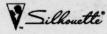

Silhouette

SPECIAL EDITION™

GOLD RUSH GROOMS

Lucky in love—and striking it rich—
beneath the big skies of Montana!

The excitement of Montana Mavericks: GOLD RUSH GROOMS continues

with

PRESCRIPTION: LOVE
(SE #1669)

by favorite author

Pamela Toth

City slicker Zoe Hart hated doing her residency in a
one-horse town like Thunder Canyon. But each time
she passed handsome E.R. doctor Christopher Taylor in
the halls, her heart skipped a beat. And as they began
to spend time together, the sexy physician became a
temptation Zoe wasn't sure she wanted to give up. When
faced with a tough professional choice, would Zoe opt to
go back to city life—or stay in Thunder Canyon with the
man who made her pulse race like no other?

Available at your favorite retail outlet.

Silhouette®

Where love comes alive™

SPECIAL EDITION™

**Don't miss the second installment in the
exciting new continuity, beginning in
Silhouette Special Edition.**

THE FORTUNES OF TEXAS: Reunion

A TYCOON IN TEXAS
by Crystal Green

Available March 2005
Silhouette Special Edition #1670

Christina Mendoza couldn't help being attracted
to her new boss, Derek Rockwell. But as she
knew from experience, it was best to keep things
professional. Working in close quarters only
heightened the attraction, though, and when family
started to interfere would Christina find the courage
to claim her love?

**Fortunes of Texas: Reunion—
The power of family.**

Available at your favorite retail outlet.

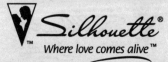

Silhouette®
Where love comes alive™

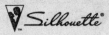

If you enjoyed what you just read,
then we've got an offer you can't resist!

Take 2 bestselling love stories FREE!

Plus get a FREE surprise gift!

Clip this page and mail it to Silhouette Reader Service™

IN U.S.A.	**IN CANADA**
3010 Walden Ave.	P.O. Box 609
P.O. Box 1867	Fort Erie, Ontario
Buffalo, N.Y. 14240-1867	L2A 5X3

YES! Please send me 2 free Silhouette Special Edition® novels and my free surprise gift. After receiving them, if I don't wish to receive anymore, I can return the shipping statement marked cancel. If I don't cancel, I will receive 6 brand-new novels every month, before they're available in stores! In the U.S.A., bill me at the bargain price of $4.24 plus 25¢ shipping and handling per book and applicable sales tax, if any*. In Canada, bill me at the bargain price of $4.99 plus 25¢ shipping and handling per book and applicable taxes**. That's the complete price and a savings of at least 10% off the cover prices—what a great deal! I understand that accepting the 2 free books and gift places me under no obligation ever to buy any books. I can always return a shipment and cancel at any time. Even if I never buy another book from Silhouette, the 2 free books and gift are mine to keep forever.

235 SDN DZ9D
335 SDN DZ9E

Name	(PLEASE PRINT)	
Address	Apt.#	
City	State/Prov.	Zip/Postal Code

Not valid to current Silhouette Special Edition® subscribers.

Want to try two free books from another series?
Call 1-800-873-8635 or visit www.morefreebooks.com.

* Terms and prices subject to change without notice. Sales tax applicable in N.Y.
** Canadian residents will be charged applicable provincial taxes and GST.
All orders subject to approval. Offer limited to one per household.
® are registered trademarks owned and used by the trademark owner and or its licensee.

SPED04R   ©2004 Harlequin Enterprises Limited

Curl up and have a

Heart *to* Heart

with

Harlequin Romance®

Just like having a heart-to-heart
with your best friend, these stories
will take you from laughter to tears
and back again. So heartwarming
and emotional you'll want to
have some tissues handy!

Next month Harlequin is thrilled to bring you
Natasha Oakley's first book for Harlequin Romance:

For Our Children's Sake (#3838),
on sale March 2005

Then watch out for....

A Family For Keeps (#3843),
by Lucy Gordon, on sale May 2005

Available wherever Harlequin books are sold.

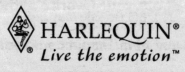

TRADING PLACES WITH THE BOSS
by Raye Morgan
(#1759) On sale March 2005

When Sally Sinclair switched roles with her exasperating boss, Rafe Allman, satisfaction turned to alarm when she discovered Rafe was not only irritating...he was also utterly irresistible!

BOARDROOM BRIDES:
Three sassy secretaries are about to land the deal of a lifetime!

Be sure to check out the entire series:

THE BOSS, THE BABY AND ME
(#1751) On sale January 2005

TRADING PLACES WITH THE BOSS
(#1759) On sale March 2005

THE BOSS'S SPECIAL DELIVERY
(#1766) On sale May 2005

Only from Silhouette Books!